REBUFF

Emmy Ellis

**Rebuff - Text copyright © Emmy Ellis 2024
Cover Art by Emmy Ellis @ studioenp.com © 2024**

All Rights Reserved

Rebuff is a work of fiction. All characters, places, and events are from the author's imagination. Any resemblance to persons, living or dead, events or places is purely coincidental.

The author respectfully recognises the use of any and all trademarks.

With the exception of quotes used in reviews, this book may not be reproduced or used in whole or in part by any means existing without written permission from the author.

Warning: The unauthorised reproduction or distribution of this copyrighted work is illegal. No part of this book may be scanned, uploaded, or distributed via the Internet or any other means, electronic or print, without the author's written permission. The author does not give permission for any part of this book to be used in Artificial Intelligence (AI).

Published by Five Pyramids Press, Suite 1a 34 West Street, Retford, England, DN22 6ES
ISBN: 9798309976508

Chapter One

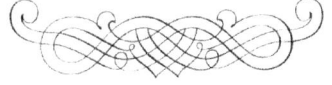

Ricky McIntyre lounged at a table in The Eagle with his father and brother, Gordon. Two blokes sat at the bar, and if he wasn't mistaken, they deliberately stared over every now and again, either annoyed with the noise going on or pissed off Ricky's family had chosen this place as their local. He missed the old pub they used to go in when he was younger, but when they'd moved back to London after years away, they hadn't been able to find somewhere to live on their old housing estate. Private rent shortage, apparently.

Living behind the factory in the small three-bed wasn't so bad. Dad and Gordon had a job there. Mum worked on the fruit and veg stall in the undercover market. Ricky was the only one left to find something. It wasn't like people advertised for thieves and killers, though, was it, and seeing as the family had moved away before because of Ricky's behaviour…

Things had changed in their absence. When they'd first come back, Dad and Gordon had been a bit gobby in the pub, establishing their presence, letting everyone know that the McIntyres were on London turf again. The thing was, Mum hadn't wanted them to draw attention to themselves, not when they'd done a runner and didn't need to stir up any old memories. Plus, Ricky still had Emma to visit. Not until the time was right, though. He'd had to lie low; he'd fucked up when they'd returned to the East End, asked around for her address, making his old mates promise not to tell her, saying he wanted to pay her a surprise visit. They'd swallowed his bullshit, and he'd stood outside her flat, ensuring she saw him. He also sent her some anonymous messages on Facebook, and he'd clearly pushed it too far because she'd guessed it was him and grassed him up to the police.

She'd actually had the balls to get hold of the coppers.

Dad hadn't been too chuffed, saying Ricky was playing with fire, considering what had gone on in the past, what Emma could reveal. A restraining order later, and he'd stopped going to her flat or messaging her, instead waiting for her in the yard of The Grey Suits where she worked. She'd gone outside in the dark for a break, and he'd let her know he was there. He hadn't found out what he needed to know, though. All right, she'd said she wouldn't tell anybody his secret because she could get into trouble for keeping it to herself, but also, *she* could get done for it because she'd been there when that fucker had taken his last breath. She hadn't murdered him, but she'd stood and watched.

She'd filmed it.

If she sent it to the police and he got arrested, he'd know it had come from her, then he'd sing, dragging her down with him. But no. Unless she was warped and didn't mind going to prison for the best years of her life, then he didn't think she was going to produce that video. Ever. He wanted it, though, and despite that stupid restraining order, he was going to get it. He'd been good since he'd last seen her in January, leaving her alone, letting her think he wasn't interested in her, but a month had gone by, Saint Valentine's Day was now a memory, and it was time for him to make contact again.

The Grey Suits, owned by The Brothers, was one of those gaffs where you got posh food for cheap. They owned another one called the Noodle or some shit like that, so he had to be careful. The last thing he wanted was either of those two up in his face. He'd heard the pair of them were just as nutty as they'd been years ago, although someone had said they were a bit more mature with it, a bit more menacing. Whatever, he didn't want to pop up on their radar, so he was going to have to play this cautiously.

Emma might well stick to her promise and not tell the police, but she might go running to the twins. Would she *really*, though, after all these years of staying silent? Would she risk them teaching her a lesson if they found out she'd witnessed a murder? She'd been so fierce and funny in their teens, up for anything, but it had all gone wrong when he'd gone too far, and their brilliant relationship had gone to shit.

"Look at that prick there," Dad said too loudly.

Ricky glanced over at the bar. One of the two men, in a garish tartan suit, played cards on the bar with a younger bloke. From what he'd gathered from earwigging, Ricky had picked up that they were called Jimmy and Sonny and they were 'security' of sorts for the landlord, Jack, and his wife, Fiona. Neither of the men looked particularly hard, but Ricky had heard that the twins were involved with this pub somehow, so Dad ought to keep his opinions to himself if he wanted to drink here.

I should have killed him ages ago.

"Just keep your head down as well as your voice," Ricky said. "We don't need the twins on our backs."

"Nor the police," Gordon said. "No thanks to you." He glared at Ricky.

Gordon had made no bones about the fact he blamed Ricky for the family moving away. Ricky was well aware it was his fault, he didn't need reminding, but Gordon seemed to think that every week or so the subject had to be brought up. How Gordon had left all of his best friends behind. How he'd been a square peg in a round hole in the village where they'd lived. And the latest one was now they'd come back, all of his old friends hadn't really been that bothered that he'd returned and nothing was the same. He'd imagined walking into a pub and being slapped on the back and man-hugged, but the kids he'd once knew were now men, some of them with families, and they weren't interested in Gordon at all.

Ricky had experienced much the same. His childhood friends had also moved on, not that he'd hung around with many because he'd chosen to spend most of his time with Emma. It was a hard thing to swallow, your mates being dismissive. They'd grown up, and they didn't want Ricky tainting their lives. He'd grown up, too, and he'd changed, but not enough to have gone to uni like Mum had suggested and sorted himself out. He still didn't have a profession other than burglary. The truth was, he couldn't be arsed with learning, had always hated school, and preferred to be his own boss.

"Why don't you just fuck off with the snide remarks?" Ricky said to Gordon. "I fucked up big time, don't you think I know that? Mum and Dad did what they thought was best and got me out of London. No one knows I did anything apart from us and Emma, and she hasn't said fuck all to anyone all these years, so I doubt very much she's likely to now."

She was the only fly in the ointment, and he planned to get rid of her, but he had to plan it carefully—or rather, go over the plans he'd already made, check them several times so he didn't mess anything up. He was going to get her onside, make her think he'd never ever kill anyone again, although she'd undoubtedly be wary of him now that he'd confronted her in the pub yard. Such a stupid thing to have done. What he was supposed to do was stand there watching her smoke, her face lighting up orange when she'd flipped the wheel of her lighter. He hadn't meant to pull on his own cigarette and alert her to the fact he was there because of the glow on the end. A dumb mistake. So were the anon messages and the loitering outside her flat.

Maybe Gordon had a point. He'd said at dinner the other night that Ricky would never learn, they'd all end up in the nick eventually. Ricky was jealous of him, to be honest. Gordon hadn't gone down the criminal route. He'd managed to stick at whatever he'd put his mind to, schoolwork, exams, then a job. Ricky's life looked chaotic compared to Gordon's, but it was going to get fixed, everything was going to be all right.

"We're not having this conversation here," Dad said. "The walls have ears."

"I wouldn't be so stupid as to bring the actual subject up," Ricky snapped.

"Are you sure about that?" Gordon sipped some of his beer.

Ricky sat with those words for a moment. Absorbed them. Accepted the truth of them. If he was going to grow and become a better person like Mum wanted, he had to know when to bite back and when to remain silent.

"I'm sorry that what I did made you have a shit time." He stared at Gordon. "I did something I regret, and I can't change it. I'm grateful we upped sticks and moved away."

"We hid out like criminals, you mean," Gordon said.

Dad nudged him with his elbow. "Did you not just hear me say the walls have ears?" He glanced over at the bar again. "Next time we come in here, we'll sit by the window so they can't hear what we're saying, but we should only be talking about this kind of thing at home."

"How can we when Mum wants to forget it?" Gordon asked. "And it was mean to bring her back here when she didn't want to come. I know how that feels because I didn't want to leave London. She made friends in Wales, she had a really good job, and now, because Ricky wanted to come back, we all came back. We all did something because of him—*again*."

"We stick together as a family," Dad said.

"So if I decided to fuck off to Ireland or somewhere like that, you're all going to follow me?" Ricky asked. "Come off it. We're not going to all live in the same fucking house for the rest of our lives just because I did something stupid in the past."

"We have to be there for each other," Dad said.

Ricky shook his head. "We still can. Even if we don't live near each other. There's a thing called a phone. Why don't you take Mum back to Wales? She's not happy here."

"*I* wasn't happy *there*," Dad grumbled.

Gordon puffed out air. "I should have stayed behind. I thought coming back here would be good, but it's shit. I hate to say it, but Ricky's right. We don't all have to stay together because of what he did. I'm going to look into fucking off back to Wales. I can't believe I just said that, considering how much I thought I hated it, but it's a damn sight better than this shithole."

Ricky nodded. "Good for you, and I'm not being sarcastic when I say that. It was my mistake, my problem. And I don't see why you three should pay." He held a hand up when his father opened his mouth to speak. "Me and Gordon aren't little anymore. We're old enough to go our own way. We don't all have to tramp around together like we would if we were kids. Just let us go."

Living in the same house was doing his nut in as well. Dad had it fixed in his head that if they stuck together then Ricky would be safe and could be persuaded to get a grip, get himself in order. Not that he wanted to turn a complete corner or anything. He enjoyed nicking shit and selling it on, and he liked the way people looked at him, sometimes unsure of whether he was going to turn on them or not. He kind of enjoyed being a menacing sort.

Maybe he should listen to Gordon. Get a proper job in the factory. Find a girl and settle down. Become Mr Anonymous. The problem with that was, Mr Know-it-All Prick still lived inside him. He hadn't grown up yet. He couldn't quite let that part of him go.

He just had to hope that wouldn't be his downfall.

Chapter Two

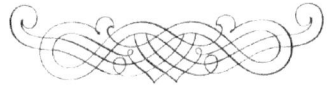

George Wilkes stared at the naked man hanging from chains attached to the cellar ceiling in their new warehouse. A few people had already been dispatched this way — three scrote drug dealers who wouldn't stick by Cardigan rules and some woman who'd abused her children. Each of them had been cut up, their body parts dropped into the choppy River Thames beneath the trapdoor in the floor. This torture room was beneath the main warehouse, stone steps leading down to it. George had got someone to place rubber treads on them as they were slippery; nobody wanted to crack their head open, did they.

"What part of paying protection money every month bypassed your brain?" he asked the fucker who'd opened a pop-up shop a couple of months ago, one of those that were sort of like a market stall. "I mean, I don't fault your business sense because shops like that where you flog everything but the kitchen sink and then fuck off again to set up elsewhere… You make a fortune, yeah? Except when our man, Martin, came and let you know you'd need to pay us some money, you decided you didn't have to, and when you buggered off, I bet you thought we wouldn't find you, didn't you?"

The man, Joe Kittering, whimpered.

"I expect your armpits are really hurting, aren't they?" George asked. "Now, this could go one of two ways. You agree to pay up, and we take you to wherever it is you keep your money so you can hand it over, or I kill you as an example. A little rumour will go around that you seem to have suddenly disappeared and it might be something to do with not paying your dues."

George wasn't sure he could trust this gimp to keep his mouth shut about what had happened here, so what he'd just said ought to be scrubbed from the record. He'd forfeit the money—it wasn't like they needed it, was it—and he'd get rid of this potential blabbermouth. He could usually suss people out pretty well. Those who were truly scared of him stood out a mile, but Kittering still had an air of entitlement about him. He didn't agree he should pay protection money, and nothing George said was going to change his mind.

George turned to Greg, who sat on a fold-out chair to watch the show.

"Is it me?" George said, "or is this prick really annoying?"

"He's really annoying."

"I thought so."

"What about his reliability in keeping his gob shut?"

"I don't think he will, bruv."

"So are we in agreement then? That even though he hasn't committed a particularly hideous crime, we need to get rid?"

"That about sums it up." Greg let out a long breath, and it clouded in the cold air.

George made a mental note to get a couple of those massive halogen heaters for down here. While the cold was a handy torture tool, he didn't much like it himself. Wearing bulky clothes under his forensic suits made it a little difficult for him to move freely when swinging a sword, axe, or any number of weapons.

He stared at Kittering's shrivelled cock and balls. There was fuck all there to get a good shot at, so he wouldn't bother. He thought about using a shooter with a silencer—noise wasn't that much of a problem as this warehouse stood by itself next to the noisy river, and after a surveillance team had watched the place for a week or so, George's previous worry that people would be around in the form of druggies selling their gear had been debunked. The area was deserted.

He sighed. He wasn't arsey enough to dive in and slash the shit out of this bloke. Yes, Kittering's audacity in not paying his bills was enough to get George's anger rising, but he wasn't in the mood to drag this out.

"Do you even care that you're going to die?" he asked. "Because from where I'm standing, you're not crying. You're not shitting yourself. You're not begging us to let you go."

"I didn't realise it would go this far."

Now Kittering looked alarmed, but it was too late in George's book. Who the fuck was so smug in front of The Brothers and expected to get away with it? Who felt they were so entitled that they could act like living by Cardigan rules wasn't even an option?

"So you realise *now*, yes?" George confirmed. "You understand that if you'd just paid us the fucking money, none of this would be happening. It's not something we negotiate on. You open a business, you pay us a wedge and we look after you. If you don't pay us, we come and find you. We asked you nicely to pay us what you owe, and I gave you a clip round the earhole as a reminder that you don't fuck us about again, which is what we've done here. You're hanging there nicely, I've kept my temper in check. It's all been amicable so far, do you agree?"

Kittering snorted. "Amicable? This?"

"Now you're getting snotty, and there's no need for it, is there?" George said. "No one likes a Billy Big balls, did anyone ever tell you that?"

"Except he hasn't got big balls," Greg said.

George smiled and stared at Kittering's wedding tackle. "I wasn't going to make reference to his shrivelled nuts, but now you come to mention it... Not such a big cock of the walk now, are we?"

Kittering closed his eyes and blew out a long, slow breath through pursed lips. Maybe this bloke was the sort who seriously thought he could do whatever he wanted, and even though he was chained up and naked, he for some reason thought he'd still get away with it.

Kittering opened his eyes, his bottom lip wobbling. "I'll pay up. I'll pay a grand on top."

George laughed. "Are we supposed to be chuffed with you popping a bit extra on what you owe? Do you realise—actually, you can't do, otherwise you'd never have offered a grand—that the daily interest rate means you owe us *twenty* grand on top? Your original bill was three hundred, one-fifty a month, and because you're an absolute prick of a bloke, you now owe twenty thousand, three hundred. We're going to let that slide—the money, I mean—because we've got a bloke stealing your car as we speak. It'll be sent abroad and sold, so your debt will be clear, but you seem a slimy cunt to me, and my brother agrees, so you're not going to be leaving here alive."

A shout of rage barked out of Kittering, and he pulled his lower half up, his arm strength impressive, then made a movement as though on a swing at the park to get himself in motion. George stepped back enough that if Kittering flashed his legs out he wouldn't get kicked.

Greg stood and moved to stand behind Kittering. He picked up the trapdoor opener—a broom handle with a loop on the end—and fed it onto a hook. The door opened, and the frantic sound of the manic river rushed in. A cold draught joined it. Greg collected the sword leaning against the wall. He didn't pass it to George but held it in a two-handed grip and swung. The blade embedded into Kittering's side, a knife through raw beef, the slice going right to his belly button. Blood welled around the metal. Greg removed the sword amid Kittering's screams, and funny enough, the bloke lost his swinging momentum. Claret coasted down over his hip and outer thigh, fucking loads of it.

Kittering stopped screaming and instead let out weird noises of pain. He clenched his teeth and breathed through his nose. Tears streamed down his face, and the amount of blood still coming out of the sword wound would mean he'd cark it soon. There was far too much liquid loss to save him.

George stepped forward and watched the blood dripping into the churning river. They'd had a chat about whether he'd use his electric saws here to chop people into slices, what with the noise it would create, and they'd done a test with Greg going outside to check whether the noise travelled. It had, but only with the trapdoor open, and against the racket of the moving river, it was faint. As nobody usually came this way, they deemed it safe, but they'd had cameras installed and a screen set up down here so they could see anyone coming. Greg switched it on then gave George the thumbs-up.

George had bought a new tool for use here—a chainsaw with a long blade so he'd have a better reach when he stood at the edge of the trapdoor and sliced people. He plugged it in and revved it up. Kittering was in no fit state to protest, although his eyes did widen slightly. George ignored him and started with the toes of one foot. They plopped into the water, and like he had in their old warehouse, he systematically dismantled this man's leg into two-inch slices. The other leg went the same way. The blades glided through the groin and torso areas easily, George cutting off thinner slices the farther up he went.

A tap on his back had him silencing the saw, and he turned to look at the CCTV monitor. A car drove past. Greg used the control panel beside the monitor to move the camera to follow the car, which parked.

A woman got out, her coat done up.

"That's all we fucking need," George said, "the RAC turning up to help her change a bastard tyre. We'll be stuck in here until they fuck off."

Greg squinted at the screen. "No we won't. That's Debbie in a new motor."

"What the fucking hell's *she* doing over here? Go and get her while I finish this tosser off."

Greg went upstairs, and George got back to work. It took another five minutes for Kittering's bits and bobs to all be under the water, floating away, fish food. George placed the saw on the tool table, shut and locked the trapdoor, and took off his protective clothing at the bottom of the stairs. He stuffed it into a black bag and carried it up into the warehouse proper. He'd have a shower before they left. His tracksuit would go in the bag, too, and he'd put on his usual grey suit.

Debbie turned to look at him when he entered. "I was just telling Greg that Moon isn't well."

George's mood deflated at the news. "What kind of unwell?"

"The kind where he needs a kidney removed."

"Oh. Shit."

"He's at the clinic now, having it done privately, and I needed…"

"You needed a cuddle." George dropped the black bag and held his arms out, hugging her while she cried against his chest. "He'll be all right. The surgeon at that clinic is the best."

"I know, but I keep… What will I do if it all goes wrong? Turns out I love the fucking bastard more than I thought."

George guided her over to a large boardroom table that would be used when other leaders came for meetings. He pushed her onto one of the chairs, then sat beside her and laid an arm over her shoulders. Greg went over to the kitchen area George had insisted on them having and got a coffee going in the Tassimo. They also had a bathroom installed, and it contained similar shelving to the old warehouse so they could store forensic suits, tracksuits, trainers, and towels, everything they needed to get cleaned up after a kill. New place, same setup.

"How long is the op?" George asked.

"There's four hours left."

"Then we should go to the Taj for lunch. That'll keep your mind off shit. We'll catch up—we haven't seen you for a good while. That's not a dig, so don't get up in arms. I just need a quick shower, then we're good to go."

"Thanks for this," Debbie said. "I knew I could count on you."

He smiled and left her with Greg, who brought her coffee over. George showered, and then they were off to the Taj, the black bag of bloodied clothes stashed in the boot ready to be burned at home later.

If there was ever a time to catch the twins red-handed, now was it. That bag made George uneasy, and regardless of the fact that he'd already ordered his lamb Rogan Josh, he excused himself and went home to dispose of it. There was no way he was going down for the murder of some little prick who hadn't paid them money. He'd rather be remembered for something more significant.

Chapter Three

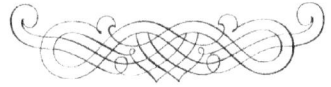

Emma had once again lapsed into a state of what she called 'uneasy contentment'. For the most part she felt okay, but there was still an edge, her nerves abraded every time she thought about Ricky. It was sad, really, how their relationship had disintegrated after the murder — or before it, to be truly honest. They'd been such good mates. They'd shared secrets, and it was such a shame it had gone to shit. Back then, she'd never imagined hating him, hating the sight of him, but now she did. All right, he'd kept away from her since that January night in the pub yard, but that might not mean anything. He might be waiting for his chance to pop up again, or maybe, if she dared to hope hard enough, he'd got the message that she really wasn't going to grass on him for what he'd done. Then again, if she'd turned to the police for a restraining order and was prepared to get him in the shit for sending her those anonymous messages, who was to say she wouldn't eventually tell them Ricky was a killer?

Then there was her cousin, Amanda, who'd had a time of it last month. Some bloke had become fixated with her, and the twins had waded in to save the day. They'd save the day regarding Ricky, too, if only Emma had the balls to ask them for help, but if she did that, it would mean admitting she'd lied to them when she'd had her interview for the job at their pub. They'd asked if she had any secrets that might jump out of the closet, and she'd said no. George had remarked that if they found out she was lying, they wouldn't be best pleased, so how the fuck could she go running to them now? How could she explain why she'd kept the murder quiet, not only because she'd been a witness, but because of her stupid, misguided loyalty to Ricky?

God, it was such a mess.

She smiled at the next customer and served them a Guinness, and as she held out the card reader for the bloke to pay for it, her smile dropped at the sight of three McIntyres coming in.

To hide her discomfort, she flashed her teeth, like she would with any other customer, and asked, "What can I get you?"

"Three lagers," Ricky said.

His dad frowned. "Is that you, Emma?"

She swerved her attention his way. "Hello, Mr McIntyre. How have you been? Haven't seen you in years."

"Not bad, not bad. You?"

"Keeping my head down." She'd said that to let him know the secret was still safe. Staring into his eyes brought back memories from the night of the murder, and she shuddered.

"That's good to hear," Mr McIntyre said. "Do you run this place or something?"

"No, but I'm doing training to become an assistant manager for when the landlord and landlady aren't here."

"Go on holiday a lot, do they?"

Why is he asking? Is he gathering info for Ricky so he can rob the place? "No, but everyone needs a day off, don't they."

"True enough. Me and Gordon have one today, but Ricky seems to have one every day. He can never stick to a job. Got any going here?"

Emma's stomach rolled over. She couldn't imagine Ricky working here, let alone putting up with him. Why couldn't they have stayed in Wales? What did they have to come back here for? Everything was going fine until then. Well, fine wasn't the right way of putting it because she'd never, ever forget the murder. She *had* put it behind her somewhat, though. She no longer woke up from crazy nightmares, and she'd packed that part of her life away in a little box, never to be opened again. Then Ricky had stood in that yard and opened it for her, forcing her to face the fact that the murder really had happened, no matter how much she'd tried to convince herself it hadn't.

"You'd have to ask Kenny or Liz." She gestured with a thumb towards the end of the bar. "They're just down there."

All three pints served, she held up the card machine. Ricky didn't produce a card, his father did, which didn't surprise her at all. Ricky had always lived by the mantra that if you could get something for free, then why not? She'd bet he'd continued his robbing ways—he never could resist putting his sticky fingers where they didn't belong. She nodded to the Mcintyres and moved along to serve someone else, relieved on one hand there was distance between them but wary on the other that they were here at all.

The men were still there an hour later, drinking pints. Hopefully they'd leave soon.

Kenny came over and stood beside Emma in a quiet moment. "I don't want to draw attention to the fact that we're talking about that bloke sitting over there, because I don't want to give them the idea you're anything to do with my decision. The one called Ricky enquired about a job. I've already said none are available but that I'll get hold of him if there are—but I doubt I will because there's something shifty about him, but I can't put my finger on it. He said you'd vouch for him, and so what I want to know is, does he always look dodgy and he's nice underneath or is he actually dodgy?"

Emma laughed to further disguise the fact they were talking about Ricky, but also because she had no idea what to say. She trusted Kenny and Liz to a certain degree, but not enough to confess to witnessing a murder and keeping her mouth shut about it. She'd never told a soul, and she didn't intend to unless she was backed into a corner.

"I've got a restraining order out against him," she said quietly, "so he shouldn't really be in here. I'd rather not cause a fuss and ask him to leave, though."

"What's happened?"

"He went weird on me and started leaving messages on Facebook from anonymous accounts. I knew it was him because of what he was saying. He was standing outside my flat a lot, too. It sounds like he was a stalker or whatever, but it isn't like that. We knew each other when we were younger. We lost touch for…reasons. I was polite enough to him when I served them because that's my job, but I don't want to work with him."

"I can turf him out if you want. He's broken the terms of the restraining order."

"If you do that, it'll make it worse. Let's just leave it for now, eh?"

"Is he making you uncomfortable by being here?"

"No," she lied. "He's not doing any harm."

"Do you think he's here to make a point?"

Yes. "No. It's just a coincidence that I happen to work here."

Kenny didn't seem convinced, but he nodded anyway. "As long as you're sure. Any trouble at all, even when you're not at work, you let me know and we'll go to The Brothers."

She smiled. "Okay."

Kenny walked off to serve Ricky's dad, and Emma glanced at the clock. It was time for her break, so she let Liz know she was off out the back for a cigarette. She purposely looked at Ricky to catch his eye and then left the bar area.

Outside, she opened the yard gate and waited on the pavement, lighting a cigarette. He appeared, as she knew he would, lighting up himself.

"Did you come here to scare me?" she asked.

"No, we're actually looking for a new local."

"You shouldn't be drinking here when there's a restraining order."

"Are you going to tell the police about it?"

"Of course not. I only went to them because you wouldn't stop it with the messages. I warned you what I was going to do and you carried on anyway. I told you, you have no problem with me. I will *not* tell anyone what you've done if you leave me the hell alone, but at the same time I had to make you see that you can't just go around trying to frighten me. I had plenty of time to grass on you when you were in Wales, but I never said a thing."

"I realise I just got a bit crazy."

"You didn't need to get crazy with me. You know me, or at least I thought you did."

"I'm sorry, all right?"

"All right. Let's put it behind us, like we said years ago."

They smoked their cigarettes in silence, and it brought home how different they were now. Years ago they'd have been chatting like no one's business, laughing their heads off about something or other, and now she didn't even want to bring up the fun times. It was best everything about their relationship was forgotten and they moved on.

She dropped her cigarette in a little puddle and then reached down to pick it up. "So are we agreed? That we're polite to each other if you come in the pub, but otherwise there's no contact?"

"There could be contact, I just need to not be a dick. If you want contact, that is."

She didn't. "I don't think it's a good idea. What we got up to, not just the murder, but all of it. We were actually delinquents, and I hate the fact that I was like that and thought it was funny. It wasn't. We were hideous."

"Yeah, I suppose we should be ashamed of ourselves."

It didn't sound like he really meant that, but she shrugged and opened the yard gate, leaving him standing there and not feeling bad about it. He was the one who'd led her down the garden path. She'd been foolish and too naïve not to follow. Now she was older and could see things for what they really were. Ricky was a manipulator, selfish, and continually out for what he could get. He was no good for her, and to be honest, she was no good for him. She swore he'd sometimes acted the way he had just to show off in front of her, to get her to like him more. They were a bad mix and were best miles apart.

But you knew that back then, too…

If the McIntyres made The Grey Suits their local and she found it too difficult to continue working there, she'd ask the twins if she could be swapped to the Noodle. They'd probably want to know why, but if she said she was moving flats then they'd understand why she needed to be on the other side of the Cardigan Estate.

Inside, she popped her drenched cigarette butt in the bin and hung her coat up in the little staffroom that contained a table and chairs and a kitchen unit with a sink, kettle, and coffee maker, plus a small set of lockers. She still had eight minutes of her break left so quickly made a cup of tea. It wouldn't be long and her shift would be over. Maybe she could go and see Amanda, stay at hers for the evening. Even overnight. She'd never confessed to her cousin about what had happened. She'd never trusted her not to tell either of their parents. It had been obvious that Amanda felt the same about Emma recently. She'd insisted their parents didn't know about Norman the stalker.

Maybe it was time that Emma proved she *did* trust her now. Did she have the guts to tell her everything? And more to the point, could she cope with the look of disgust that was sure to drench Amanda's face? She doubted it.

Tea made, she sat at the table and managed to drink half of it before her time was up. She took the cup with her behind the bar so she could sip it in between serving customers. The McIntyres remained at the table, the dad and Gordon in deep conversation, but Ricky sat with his head bent, and he fiddled with his fingers. She got on with her job, putting him to the back of her mind. Well, she sorted out the logistics of moving closer to the Noodle if that family now lived in this area. She wouldn't be telling any of their mutual friends where she lived either. None of them had kept their mouth shut last time when he'd asked them for her address.

Or was it time for her to leave London like the McIntyres had? Maybe removing herself from the equation would put an end to this bullshit once and for all.

Chapter Four

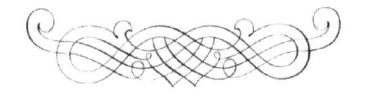

There was no other way to describe how she felt about him. She was obsessed. There was something about Ricky that pulled her in. They say opposites attract, and in this case that was true. Emma was a good girl and Ricky was a bad boy. He acted up and thought nothing of annoying people for fun. He'd always annoyed her before; she'd tutted when he'd

interrupted a teacher explaining something or he butted into a conversation she was having with Amanda, but he'd grown on her somehow, ever since they'd gone to the same birthday party together. That was the thing at the moment, everyone having parties, the next one outdoing the last. But they weren't in houses, it had to be a venue, like hiring the local hall or going to the cinema or bowling. She supposed it made you feel grown up to do that rather than have everyone at your house eating jelly and ice cream, and they were way past pass the parcel now.

The point Emma had seen Ricky in a different light was when they'd sat next to each other in a corner of the function room in a pub where Sasha North was having her sixteenth. She was one of the oldest in their year and always managed to look about eighteen. It was probably the makeup. Anyway, Ricky had received a message, and Emma had had a sly peek. He had a text from his mum saying to be careful when he got home because his dad wasn't in a good mood. Ricky had asked his mother if she was okay, and she'd said she was, and he'd responded with "I love you". In Emma's experience, kids their age would never admit to saying that to one of their parents, and when he'd caught her watching, he'd shrugged and said, "Well, I do."

It had been weird to match that with the boy she'd known him as before then. If she viewed him honestly, he was a bully and a relentless tease.

"I'm going home."

He'd stood, and she'd got up, too, following him out into the rain-drenched night. He hadn't even asked what she was doing as they'd walked along together, Emma texting Amanda to let her know she was getting the bus home because she wasn't feeling very well. Even then, she'd known not to mention Ricky, so she supposed, deep down, she knew being with him wasn't the right thing for her.

Ever since that night, they'd met up after school and he'd walked her to the end of her street. She thought about him constantly, or that's what it felt like anyway, her head stuffed with Ricky this and Ricky that. At first she'd found it difficult to hide what she was up to from her family. She'd always hung around with Amanda previously, and if she stopped it completely then there were going to be questions, so Emma was prepared to meet up with her on Monday nights, claiming she had a lot of studying to do for her exams. That wasn't a lie, but she was grateful she had the kind of brain where she only ever had to read things a couple of times and it stuck. That meant she didn't have to cram excessively, although her parents thought she did. Emma had made up some bullshit that she was round a friend's house every evening to study, but most of the time she roamed the streets with Ricky.

How weird that she was doing things she never thought she would. Things she'd sworn *she wouldn't, the biggest one being that she hung around with 'one of those boys' who would get her into trouble one day, 'you mark my words'.*

She was starting to not give shit about that.

Funny how what she knew was wrong didn't matter and she was doing it anyway. Not funny to her parents if they ever found out, though. Amanda had been asking questions as to why they didn't walk home together anymore, because Emma had been leaving as quickly as possible so she could be with Ricky. She'd told Amanda she'd wanted to get home quickly as Amanda tended to dawdle... That excuse had been accepted. Amanda had no reason to believe Emma was changing. Emma doubted anyone *would believe she was changing as much as she was. Sometimes, she couldn't believe it herself.*

Every now and then she wanted to listen to the little voice in her head and break things off with Ricky before it went too far. She longed to be who she was, but at the same time longed to be whoever waited for her in her future life. She wasn't stupid. Aligning herself with Ricky was a mistake, but every time she rehearsed what she'd say to him in a breakup speech, it always set her off crying. And anyway, it wasn't breaking up because they weren't together like that, they'd just become really good friends. The stuff they talked about was dark and weird and disturbing, stuff that to begin with, when Ricky had brought it up, had shocked her. Her first instinct had been to recoil, to get away from him, a warning bell going off, her mum's voice saying, "What on earth do you think you're doing with him, Emma?" But then he'd laughed and said he was joking and it was okay to talk about it as long as you didn't do it.

What was their conversation going to be about tonight?

She was on her way to meet him at the park. They never sat on the swings or whatever but inside a cluster of trees that had a hole in the top so they could lie back and stare at the sky while they chatted their nonsense. They had to whisper in case other kids were hanging around, but they seemed to know not to bother coming into the den because it was Ricky's. She tried to understand how everybody just knew what to do when it came to him. Maybe because he gave off predator vibes and those weaker ones who'd be his prey understood the unspoken rules.

It was kind of good to be the only person he hung around with on a regular basis. No one had gone back and told Amanda about the unlikely friendship yet, but Emma already had her story straight, that Ricky was good underneath it all and they actually studied together. Amanda would never believe it, so Emma was going to have to give it a really good go in convincing her that was the truth. Anyway, so long as she didn't change how she acted so no one could accuse Ricky of influencing her, everything would be all right.

She reached the trees and dipped her head beneath the low-hanging branches. He was already there, sitting on a large crinkled piece of tarpaulin he must have bought in his backpack, a little torch on beside him.

"Thought you weren't going to bother coming," he said.

He always did that, sounding like he was telling her off, as if he was her parent instead of a kid she hung around with. At the beginning it had scared her, his snark, and she'd been quick to reassure him she'd always meet him unless she was grounded, but tonight a prickle of irritation gripped her. She reckoned it was because she hadn't let him brainwash her to the degree that she couldn't see who he was and what was going on. What was he doing now, trying to guilt trip her because she was about two minutes late?

She sat beside him. "Get a grip."

He laughed, probably to cover up any embarrassment because she'd called his bluff—or, as he'd likely see it, she'd stood up to him. She waited for an admonishment, for him to tell her to rein it in, that you didn't speak to Ricky McIntyre like that, but he didn't. He lay back, the tarpaulin crumpling beneath him, and looked at the stars.

"What did you have for dinner?" he asked.

So the danger was over, then.

She flung herself back and put her hands behind her head. "Lasagne and chips, then we had jam roly-poly and custard for pudding. What about you?"

"Sausage and chips—jumbo sausages—and I wanted to slide a whole one down my dad's throat and block his windpipe, then squeeze his nostrils together so he couldn't breathe."

So it was going to be one of those evenings, and that was okay. Emma had long got over the shock of what Ricky liked to talk about. To be honest, she used it as a form of therapy to get all the bad feelings out of her when they discussed killing people who pissed them off. There was no way she'd ever do it, of course there wasn't, but they were only words, and seeing as only

Ricky heard them, they weren't hurting anyone, were they.

"What's he done this time?" she asked.

"Mum's got another bruise on her wrist."

"Why doesn't she leave him?"

"I don't know."

If Emma was asked that question, she wouldn't be able to explain why she wouldn't leave Ricky either. All right, she wasn't in a relationship like his parents, she had to keep reminding herself of that, but Ricky still had a hold on her. She still found herself doing whatever he wanted, even if she knew it was wrong. It was nights like these she preferred the most, where they hid themselves away and didn't get up to anything stupid. But when Ricky was in the mood to go out on the streets… God, the things she'd seen him get up to. It was mainly nicking stuff or damaging something — kicking a rubbish bin so everything flew out onto the path or knocking over a bollard on a road island, then they'd run away, laughing their heads off. She'd admit she got a thrill out of it, that she felt more alive than she did usually. Being a teenager was a completely different experience when she spent her time with Ricky.

It would end one day, when someone really pretty caught his attention. He'd stop hanging around with

Emma, and she wasn't entirely sure what she'd do. Go back to being her old self, the one she pretended to be anyway? It kind of worried her, this track they were on. How she was prepared to lie so easily so her mum and dad had no idea who she was becoming.

How strange to know it was wrong but to do it anyway.

Chapter Five

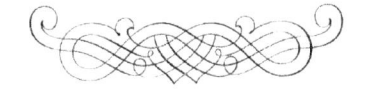

Meryl McIntyre had bloody loved Wales, and if she wasn't so wary of her husband, Verne, she'd have refused to return to London. It was such a shame. She'd settled so well in the village, making friends, feeling completely at home. More at home than she ever had in the Big Smoke. She should have done what she'd wanted to and left before the murder—left Verne. That kid Ricky had killed would still be alive, and any potential pointing fingers towards her son wouldn't have existed. But she'd jumped in and made the best of a terrible situation, and those years in the village had more community spirit than she'd ever experienced in London.

It had become easier and easier to pretend the murder hadn't happened, though. The more days that passed, the more she'd convinced herself that Ricky was as innocent as the day he'd been born. If it wasn't for Verne being an arsehole, she could have claimed her life was as close to Heaven as she could get without being six feet under.

Her family was out on the piss today, a tradition she didn't much like. Her dad had done it, Verne's dad had done it, and her husband was passing it on to their sons. Gordon wasn't particularly enamoured with sitting in a pub all day once or twice a month. He reckoned it was a waste of time when he could be gaming online with his mates back in Wales, but of course, Ricky was up for it, anything so he didn't have to work.

She smiled at a customer coming towards the fruit and vegetable stall that she currently manned alone. The woman who owned it had taken herself off for lunch at the nearby café. The customer stopped short as though she'd seen a ghost, and now Meryl had a moment to study her properly, she cottoned on it was the mother of that lad Ricky had killed. Fucking hell. What was she supposed to do now? What should she say? She'd given her condolences when it had happened, so wouldn't it be weird to bring it up now? Wouldn't it make her look guilty by association?

"What can I get you, love?" she said, slapping on a smile.

Clare Donaldson hesitated for a second longer and then stepped forward, jittery, as if shaking off a ghostly cloak from the past. Shit, did that mean she'd suspected Ricky all those years ago? As far as Meryl knew, all the kids had been spoken to by the police, not just Ricky. Maybe their mass exodus to Wales had drawn attention, people gossiping about their departure and coming up with theories that were far too close to the truth. Yet the police hadn't contacted them again, and it had said online that someone in the homeless community had done it. The dead lad's phone had been taken, as had a Mars bar and a packet of crisps in his coat pocket, not to mention a few quid he had on him.

"A couple of pounds of grapes, the green ones, and eight Granny Smith," Clare said. She'd sounded stiff so clearly had a beef.

Meryl got on with weighing the grapes. "How have you been?"

"About as happy you'd expect when your son's been killed."

"Bless you, it was such a terrible time." Meryl put the grapes in a brown bag and twisted it closed. Was it obvious her hands were shaking?

Clare sniffed. "And a guilty time, I should imagine, for those who knew what really happened."

Meryl counted out the apples. "Oh, definitely. At least the homeless man went to prison for it."

"I now don't believe it was him."

Meryl's stomach rolled over, but she pretended everything was fine, passing over the two brown bags. "Oh blimey. I wasn't aware anyone else was in the frame. We'll call it four quid for all the fruit."

Clare handed over a fiver. "Oh yes, I believe the culprit is closer to home."

Was she implying it was closer to *Meryl's* home? She'd have to nip that in the bud pretty sharpish. "But there was no way it would be you or your family. That's just daft."

"I didn't mean *that* home." Clare took the pound change Meryl held out and dropped it in her jacket pocket. She picked up the brown bags and cradled them to her chest. "I don't know how you live with yourself."

She strutted off, Meryl staring after her. Her whole world had just tumbled down around her. Clare knew, she fucking well knew somehow, and Meryl would bet that woman wouldn't rest until she'd brought the truth to light. Now Clare had seen Meryl, did that mean it would give her a renewed sense of determination to prove Ricky had killed her son? Would there be a tap on the door one day, something Meryl had dreaded for years? Her eyes stung, and she was about to allow herself a good cry when the stall owner returned from lunch.

"Off you go then," Mrs Brown said.

Meryl nodded and made her way to the café, glancing this way and that in case Clare hovered nearby, waiting to have a set-to now she'd had the courage to speak when she'd bought the fruit.

Meryl burst into the café and swept it with a glance, relieved Clare wasn't there. She ordered a pie, mash, and garden peas with gravy, starving because she hadn't had any breakfast. Maybe she wasn't normal to be able to eat in these circumstances, but if she didn't have her usual full meal, the woman behind the counter would notice and say something.

Meryl couldn't be doing with the hassle.

She took the tray of tea and sat in the corner at the back, waiting for her lunch to be brought over. She scanned the other customers, then looked out into the covered market. Clare wasn't at the bric-a-brac stall opposite, so Meryl relaxed a bit. She should message Verne, really, and let him know what had been said, but he'd have had at least four or five pints by now and she couldn't risk him getting lairy and shouting the odds. He'd probably storm round to the Donaldson house and create a fuss. But wasn't it better that there was a retaliation rather than the McIntyres keeping quiet as though they were guilty? Which they were. All of them had played various roles, and in a court of law, all of them would be classed as culpable after the fact. They'd be put in prison.

Had Emma opened her mouth to Clare? Had she finally caved from the pressure of her conscience and confessed? No, that couldn't be right. Clare Donaldson wasn't the type to keep this quiet. She'd have marched Emma down to the police station and forced her to tell the coppers what had gone on.

I'm just being paranoid.

Meryl's lunch arrived, and she tucked in, thinking over when she'd tell Verne about what had happened. It couldn't be first thing because he'd have an unholy hangover—he wasn't good in the morning at the best of times, let alone when he'd had a skinful. He had another day off and likely planned to spend it lying on the sofa watching telly. She also had a day off in lieu of working Saturdays. Maybe she could persuade him to go out for a walk. They could go down by the river where no one was around and she could tell him what Clare had implied, safe in the knowledge that no one would overhear their conversation.

Or him spouting off after she'd told him.

Meryl had often imagined being Clare, but what she couldn't imagine was the sheer force of emotion that must have hit that poor woman upon hearing that her son had been killed. To know that she would never see him again, or hear him, or feel his hand on her arm. Meryl would have to pretend that either of her boys had gone away if something awful happened to them. She'd tell herself they'd moved to Australia and cut contact, anything so she wouldn't have to face the truth.

As a mother of a murderer, she'd had to come to terms with the fact that her eldest son was a wrong 'un. She'd had warning enough as Ricky had been growing up that he wasn't normal. He didn't think the same way as other people. Getting a proper job was for mugs; it was easier to steal. Doing something productive of an evening, like going to the youth club or sitting around a mate's house playing board games, had never been on his radar. He'd preferred loafing around the streets, Emma glued to his side, and sometimes they'd met up with a group of lads who'd stolen alcohol from their parents' houses and cigarettes from whoever happened to have a packet they could get their thieving hands on.

I didn't want him to grow up like that. I didn't want him to take away someone else's life and not even be bothered about it.

That was the bit she couldn't get her head around. Ricky had no remorse. The only thing that seemed to trouble him was that Emma had recorded what he'd done. She'd promised she'd got rid of the footage. There was no way that girl was going to grass on Ricky when it meant she'd be involved, too.

Meryl wasn't proud of her part in the coverup, but she was proud of her dedication to being a mother. No one could accuse her of not going to the ends of the earth for her eldest son, and she was doing the same thing now by returning to London when she hadn't wanted to. She and Gordon had been so happy in Wales that she sometimes wondered whether he'd go back with her if she suggested it. But she was too afraid of Verne to even suggest returning to her beloved little village. Ricky had wanted to go back to London, and Verne had taken the decision out of her hands and made arrangements for them all to go.

If it wasn't for the secret, she could have stayed behind. But there *was* a secret, one she might not be able to run from for much longer if Clare Donaldson had got the bit between her teeth.

Chapter Six

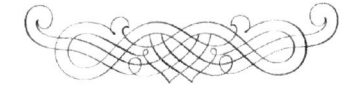

Ricky had slowed it right down with the drinking, switching to non-alcoholic lager without telling his dad. He'd get the piss taken out of him for it, but he didn't want to get too drunk, even though he acted as if he already was. In reality, he'd only had two alcoholic lagers when they'd first come into the Suits. He wasn't in the mood to get trollied anyway, he had shit to think about.

The annoying thing was he believed Emma. She wasn't about to go running off to the police. Thankfully, Dad agreed, although he was reluctant at first. Gordon thought they were safe with her, and Mum had always been her champion and said she'd never grass them all up, so as there didn't appear to be any reason to worry, what the fuck was Ricky still doing here? He could be out robbing, making some cash instead of sitting with his brother and father slurring their words and getting right on his tits.

He glanced over at the bar. Emma had her coat on, so was she going out again for a smoke? She wasn't looking his way, so he quickly nipped out the front door and ran around the back. He waited on the corner by the yard wall, not wanting her to see him this time if she opened the gate. Mind you, if she was on a break, she'd stay in the yard and he'd see her cigarette smoke puffing into the sky.

The creak of the gate had him dipping his head back so he wasn't seen, and he prayed she didn't come this way. Footsteps tapped on the pavement, but it sounded as if they were going away from him rather than towards. He popped his head round. There she was, walking down the street. He followed, keeping back, his footsteps light and in time with hers. She didn't look over her shoulder, nor did she pick up her pace, so she couldn't have sensed him behind her. She crossed the street and went past the end of another, then she disappeared down an alley. By the time he got there, she was gone. He ran down it and out the other end, but the street was blocks of four houses with alleys in between, and she could have gone down any one of them.

He frowned because he wasn't in the area where she lived. If she was going home, she'd have gone the other way and bumped straight into him when he'd been hiding around the corner. Did she have a boyfriend? He hadn't picked that information up on his travels. The only reason he cared whether she had one was the man might prove to be a nuisance. Maybe he should go back to the pub and ask Kenny if Emma was available, like, was she single. Would that look weird, too forward? Or did men ask that sort of thing all the time? Maybe he could get Gordon to do it.

Annoyed she'd got away from him so easily, he returned to the pub and finished off his warm pint, Dad and Gordon so wrecked they probably hadn't even noticed he'd gone out. And you'd think they'd be more vigilant around him, wouldn't you, considering what he'd done, but they clearly believed he wouldn't do anything like that again.

But he thought about it. Killing Emma. Getting rid of the link to the past.

Killing Dad.

"Fuck this shit," he muttered and got up. "I'm off."

Dad roared with laughter. "Fucking lightweight."

"Whatever."

Ricky barged out of the pub and headed for the bus stop. He'd catch a ride to the covered market and meet Mum when she'd finished work. He wanted to talk to her about Emma. She'd always been good at putting his mind at rest, and if he relayed what had been going on since they'd got back from Wales, yes she'd tell him off for sending the anonymous messages and standing outside her flat, but she'd understand.

He arrived just as she was pulling down the shutters on the front of the built-in stall. She padlocked it and said goodbye to the owner, and then she caught sight of him and her smile faded. She was normally happy to see him, so it was a shock that she wasn't. She glanced around, acting odd, then walked up to him and looped her arm around his, taking him out of the market.

"Thank God I've got someone to talk to. Please tell me you're not drunk."

"No, I had two pints hours ago. Dad and Gordon are fucked, though. What's the matter? What's happened?"

"We'll talk about it down by the river."

"Do I need to be worried?"

"I bloody well hope not."

She went on to talk about some of the customers she'd spoken to today, banal shit he wasn't interested in, but he understood she was filling the time until they reached the river. Once they did, she sat on a bench and stared out at the water which looked black and so deep from their spot behind the railings.

"So tell me," he said.

"Clare Donaldson came to the stall today."

His stomach rolled over.

"I could tell she didn't want to be there once she realised it was me behind the stall. Maybe seeing me was a shock. Who knows? But it was like she'd been kicked in the teeth. I didn't know how to act. I swear to God, the amount of times I've imagined seeing that woman again, and this was not how I expected it to go. I asked her what she wanted, and it was grapes and apples, all very normal, and then she implied that the killer was closer to home, my home, and I reckon she thinks it was you."

"Shit."

"I know, and I've been trying not to worry but I can't help it. I even imagined Emma had spoken to her, but if that was the case, can you see Clare keeping her mouth shut and not going to the police in order to protect Emma?"

"No. Maybe I was wrong to want to come back to London."

"I bet Clare's seen you and it stirred up old memories. She's thought of something, and it's pointed her in your direction."

"Then why hasn't she gone to the coppers?"

"Maybe she has and they don't think she's right. Or maybe they're investigating it. They might need time before they ask you any questions. I think you should leg it."

"I knew you would. There'll be some out there who would have called the police on me years ago and they wouldn't have been wrong."

"But it was an accident. Self-defence."

How could self-defence be thirty-two stab wounds in the back? It would never stand up in court.

"Actually, it's best I don't run. It'll make me look guilty. We should just act normal and see what happens," he said. "I've seen Emma today, and honest to God, she isn't a threat."

"I never thought she was. It was your dad who—"

"Yeah, well, he has loads of opinions that aren't right, like dragging you and Gordon back to London when you didn't want to come. You should have stood your ground and stayed there. You earned enough to pay all the bills on your own, and now look, you can't get a job in the same profession because there's none going and you're reduced to standing behind a market stall."

"Don't knock it, son, a job is a job, and I'm just grateful I'm earning. Doesn't matter where it is so long as the money's coming in. I thought about going back earlier—to Wales, I mean. Just packing my stuff. I'd stay with Joan."

"I like her, she was a good neighbour."

"She'd probably let me live there permanently now her husband's gone. The poor cow doesn't deserve to be a lonely widow."

Ricky put his hand around his mum's shoulders. "Then go. I'll handle Dad."

"He'll come and get me. He'd drag me back by my hair. You heard what he said that night when we got home. I'm stuck with him."

"But if you think about his threat, it's bullshit. There's no way you could have committed the murder because you were at home with Gordon."

"It's the afterwards bit I'm worried about. We *all* went to see that lad's body. I sometimes think your father made us go as a family so he'd always have a hold over us. Emma being there, too, was a necessity."

"I know what he's like," Ricky said. "And if you ever need to talk about it… I've heard what he says, and I've seen him a couple of times with his hand around your throat and his fist up in the air. You should have left him years ago when we were little." He hated himself for the way that had come out. "Sorry, that sounded as if I was blaming you. What I meant was I wish you'd had the courage to leave him. Even if you'd left us behind, we'd have been all right. He was never horrible to us, but you…"

He couldn't look at her. She'd be crying, letting out the tension she'd always held inside for as long as he could remember. And maybe she'd be crying because her abusive marriage hadn't been a secret all along. She maintained the façade that they were a strong family unit and her husband loved her to distraction, when really he ordered her around and threatened her. He hurt her. Especially when he was drunk. God knows what else he'd said to her regarding the family's viewing of the body, but him telling her he could pin it on her if she stepped out of line had been bad enough.

"Yes, you should go," he reiterated. "Phone Joan, get the ball rolling. See if you can have your old job back before you put your eggs in one basket. But I promise you, I *will* handle Dad."

And it would be so easy to do that. Was Mum aware that Dad had been shagging some woman called Karla in a B&B room down the Pigeon's Nest? Gordon had let slip that Karla had been getting a bit too friendly with Dad at work, and Ricky had got suspicious when Dad had gone out for the evening without either him or Gordon, saying he had mates he was meeting up with. It had to be bollocks because Dad had never done that since they'd come back from Wales. The hunch had been right. Ricky had followed him, seen him at the bar in the Pigeon's with some tart about his age. They'd gone through a door at the back about half an hour later, and Ricky had walked in to ask where it led to.

"Rooms upstairs. Would you like to book one?" the barmaid had said.

"Book one? Like overnight?"

"Or for an hour or two, it's up to you."

So it was *that* kind of place. Ricky had waited outside in the bus stop overhang opposite, hunched up in his puffa jacket with the hood up so he was less recognisable, a scarf over the lower half of his face. Dad and Karla had come out three hours later, Ricky frozen and livid, those two laughing on a post-sex high.

He hadn't told his mother because he didn't want her upset. Plus, he didn't want her to confront Dad who'd use his fists in response, and this time, because Dad would feel so angry, Mum might end up in hospital.

"How will you handle him?" she asked.

"You don't need to worry about that." With his arm still across her shoulder, Ricky gave her a squeeze. "You just leave that bastard to me." He was going to have to do it so his mother wasn't suspected of anything. "Don't speak to Joan until… Just not yet. There'll be plenty of time to get it all sorted."

"You don't sound right, and it's worrying me."

"Do you love him?"

"Not anymore."

"Do you mean that?"

"Of course I bloody do, otherwise I wouldn't have said it."

"Then I'll fix everything."

She turned to him and gripped the front of his coat in her fist. "Don't do anything to draw attention to yourself. Please…"

"I'll try not to." And that was as much of a promise as he was prepared to make.

Chapter Seven

Emma's heart thudded so hard then lost a beat. It frightened her because it felt like her chest had gone completely hollow for a moment, but then the beats sped up, and a flush of adrenaline flooded her system.

Ricky had set fire to some newspapers in a couple of old oil drums down the street where the homeless congregated. None of the tramps were in their usual places where they leaned on the low wall in front of a graveyard. They were likely all off begging in the busier areas, so she felt safe with no witnesses around. Unless somebody stood behind the dark windows of the building opposite. Although from the look of it, the place was abandoned. One of the panes had a large, jagged hole in it, and the ghostly shape of a pigeon stood behind it.

"Why don't the homeless go and live in there?" She studied the dancing flames that licked the air.

Ricky glanced over at the building and shrugged. "Let's go and have a look, see if we can get in."

They crossed the street and entered an alley bordered by high brick walls, and halfway down on the left, a black gate with peeling paint and a circular handle made of metal that had rusted. Ricky curled his gloved fingers through the handle and turned it. Emma winced, waiting for it to make a squeaking sound, but it didn't; the gate swung open silently. She followed Ricky into a cobbled yard, the stones shiny from recent rain. A lamppost looked as though it peeped over the brick wall to the far right, its orange glow illuminating old, broken wooden pallets laid out haphazardly.

She closed the gate behind them and whispered, "The tramps could be using that wood to keep warm. I don't get why they haven't nicked it or why they don't doss in there at night."

"The place might look abandoned, but someone could come every day and they know it. Maybe they were using it and they got turfed out so they stay over the road instead."

Emma didn't understand it. If she was homeless, then her first priority, especially in this rain, would be to find shelter regardless of whether she'd been told she couldn't stay somewhere. And when it was so clearly abandoned, standing there doing nothing, what was the harm in a few people kipping there?

Ricky had walked off to a door. She reckoned this used to be some kind of factory, the red bricks grubby, black in places from years of London grime. A padlock kept the door shut, so the owner must have assumed the homeless wouldn't bother trying to get hold of any bolt cutters. They weren't about to beg for money for a tool when they needed food and water—and drugs, so Mum had said once when they'd walked past someone begging in town.

Despite the lock, Ricky lowered the handle, and the door swung inwards. "A deterrent, that's all. Most people see a padlock and they wouldn't try to get in."

"Anyone would if they were desperate enough."
"Come on."

She went inside after him. He switched on the little torch he always kept in his pocket, and she shut the door, thinking that the light would be seen even though the windows were filthy. All right, it would only be the homeless if they'd come back to their patch, and they'd perhaps think the owners were inside, using a torch because the electricity had been cut off, but she didn't like the idea of someone knowing they were in here. She preferred to do things on the quiet, which was why Ricky setting fire to the newspapers had given her an uneasy feeling.

She couldn't have her 'nice Emma' image ruined by it getting out she was a cow from time to time. So why was she hanging around with Ricky? The longer she did, the more likely she'd be found out.

He disappeared into a room on the right, the one behind the scattered pallets. She walked over to the window, her trainers scuffing what appeared to be torn bits of paper, maybe something put down beneath underlay and carpet back in the day. She looked at the filthy window, but it was cleanish on this side, it was just the outside muck that obscured the view. She turned to view the room. Ricky stood in the far corner, shining his torch light on a dead mouse.

"Gross," she said.

"It's got maggots coming out of its stomach."

That meant there'd been flies, and there'd be a damn sight more once those maggots hatched. She'd always thought flies only came out in the summer, but what did she know? She shuddered at the thought of more mice—alive ones that scurried. She wanted to leave, but if she told Ricky that, then he'd laugh and called her a chicken. One part of her didn't care if he did, but another, much bigger part told her to stay put and prove to him she could be just as tough as he was.

"Let's go and find some more," she said, the words out before her real self could stop them. "If we had a BB gun, we could shoot them."

Ricky swung round, the torch beam following his movement and spotlighting her. She blinked at the brightness.

"Fucking hell, I'm going to be seeing white spots for a while now." She shielded her eyes and casually slouch-walked out to wait for him in the corridor.

He led the way to the next door along but on the opposite side. Once again at the window, she stared through a relatively clean patch at smoke coming from the tops of the oil drums instead of flames. A homeless bloke sat between them, his back against the low wall. The larger of the gravestones stuck up like broken teeth behind him, the light of a Victorian lamppost illuminating them from its position beside the door of a squat stone building that she assumed was used by whoever worked at the graveyard. A church stood in the distance, and it struck Emma as a bit mean that the God followers hadn't extended their so-called Christian generosity towards the raggedy men who slept on the periphery of their pious little world. They only had to glance this way to see a row of tousle-haired heads above the wall or, if the men were lucky, beanie hats.

She had to turn away. She was as guilty as those in the church for pretending the homeless didn't exist. Mum said you couldn't trust them anymore, they weren't like the homeless in her day when you knew damn well if someone sat on the street then they were desperate. A new breed of criminal had sprung up, people who got dressed in scutty clothes on purpose and put dirt or whatever on their faces to make them look like they lived on the streets. That wasn't something Mum could ignore if ever she came down here at night. Emma had seen at least four men at a time huddled together, trying to sleep.

Next time they came this way, she was going to give them some money.

They explored the rest of the building. A couple of big rooms at the back had rows and rows of tables, or maybe they would be called workbenches, and one of them had a sewing machine on top. Emma assumed the rest had been taken away to be sold off and this one had been left behind because it was broken. But she had no trouble seeing what this place had been like when it had life in it. It was a shame the business had closed down.

They moved upstairs where they found some mice in a nest made of what Emma thought was that paper from downstairs. She imagined the mummy mouse going up and down, up and down until she'd made a place for her babies. The mother lay at the back of the nest, the little ones new—they didn't even have any hair on them yet, and their eyes were closed, showing through the thin skin as black balls.

Ricky stamped on the nest.

It took all of Emma's strength not to make a sound, but what he'd done was horrific, worse than anything she'd seen him do so far. He'd killed those animals for no reason. He turned to look at her, his foot still on the nest, and she shrugged as if it didn't bother her. He took his foot away and smiled that weird little smile he always did when she'd maybe surprised him with her reaction.

Now he was going to think she was like him and she was prepared to kill animals. If they found more mice and he told her to stamp on them, would she? No, she'd tell him he should do it because she liked to watch. God, that sounded so weird.

They traipsed through a series of rooms that were likely for the staff. A fair few had wooden desks in them and metal filing cabinets covered in a layer of dust. A large one was obviously where the staff had eaten their lunch—lots of Formica-topped tables and orange plastic chairs. At the end, an open hatch and a kitchen beyond, so loads of people must have worked here.

"I know I said it earlier, but I still don't get why those blokes out there aren't using this place. There aren't even druggies or squatters dossing about."

"Who cares?"

Emma pushed open the last door in the corridor, finding herself in a square space with three doors ahead. Plaques displayed images of a stick man, a woman, and a wheelchair. She went into the women's. At the back, a row of about twenty toilets in stalls. To her right, three showers, and three rails in the shape of a U where curtains must have hung. To the left, five sinks. She moved to the closest shower and turned the metal knob, her glove slippery on the surface. A pained groan in the pipe, and then water cascaded out.

"Fucking hell," she said, "they could even get washed. The water's cold, but still…"

"You'll be telling me you're going to petition for this to be made into a homeless shelter or something soon."

"Why not? And it's a good thing to do. It would at least bring attention to an empty building and the fact that homeless people sleep outside."

"Who wants to do good, though?"

He'd sounded as if he really meant that, too, like he was puzzled someone would actually want to help those blokes. It confused her because he could do nice things like asking his mum if she was all right and telling her he loved her, and he watched out for her a lot because of his dad, so why was her suggestion any different? Or did he struggle with helping people outside his family? Did he think that wanting to make a stranger's life better was a waste of time?

"I suppose." She'd learned to appease him, to make out she agreed with everything he said, rather than have a debate about it because it wouldn't be a healthy one. It would turn into him getting stroppy and then trying to manipulate her into seeing it his way.

It was so fucking odd to know he was an arsehole, and yet she couldn't stop herself from meeting with him every night. What was she hoping for? That he would see her as someone other than a buddy and kiss her? Tell her she meant more to him than anyone else they kicked about with? Okay, that wasn't often, they tended to fuck around on their own most of the time, so she kind of had her answer really, didn't she? He must *like her more than the others. It annoyed her that it mattered so much when she had Amanda, who liked her more than anyone else they'd ever hung around with. But Amanda was like a best friend, she'd always been there. They never did anything exciting, yet Ricky was up for anything, and there was never a dull moment, unless you counted the times they lay in the tree clearing and didn't speak.*

"I'm bored now," she said, knowing damn well that would make him think of something naughty to do, which hopefully involved getting out of here and going somewhere else. Now he'd shut down her imagination to transform this place for people who needed it, she didn't want to be here.

He pissed her on her cornflakes a lot, and she'd asked herself before whether that was because he wanted to stop her from thinking for herself so he was the only one who came up with the great ideas.

They left the building but didn't go back down the alley towards the graveyard. She was glad; then she wouldn't see the smoking oil drums and that man sitting between them, trying to get warm from the heat trapped in the metal. They went the other way, past an area where shady deals could go down, the sort of seedy she didn't want anything to do with. She chucked out a laugh at that. Ricky was the sort of seedy she shouldn't want anything to do with, yet here she was.

"What are we going to do next?" she asked.

"Dunno, we'll see what crops up."

Which meant he didn't have a clue, so he hadn't planned the evening beyond setting fire to the oil drums, which he'd announced as soon as she'd met up with him.

They ended up down by the river, sitting on the wall with their legs dangling over the other side beneath the lowest rung of the railing. Emma hung her arms over the middle one, and she pretended she was caged in like she would be on a roller coaster. She closed her eyes and imagined being on a ride, dipping and swooping and doing a loop-the-loop, her stomach rolling over for real because she could see it as though it was really happening.

"Do you see shit in your head?" She opened her eyes to look across at him where he stood beside her.

"What do you mean?"

"Well, I just pretended I was on a roller-coaster ride and I could see the track, the sky, the rest of the fairground, everything."

"Um, nope."

"So when you imagined killing your dad with the jumbo sausage, what did you see?"

"Nothing. I just knew that's what I wanted to happen."

Emma couldn't fathom not seeing things inside her head, and as Ricky looked really pissed off, as though she'd just proved to him she was far superior in the imagination department, she reckoned it was best to change the subject, otherwise he'd get arsey.

Why do I hang around with someone who makes me walk on eggshells?

"How come you've got a beef with Spencer?" she asked.

"Dunno."

He said that a lot, dunno, and she thought it was so he had time to think of an answer.

"He dogs me off, that's all," he said. *"You know when you just don't like the look of someone's face and you want to punch it?"*

"Yeah." She wasn't even pretending with that one, because surely *everyone* experienced that feeling.

"That," he confirmed.

"And there's nothing else?"

"Nope."

What a really stupid reason to pick on someone. Spencer was just a quiet kid, like Emma had been before Ricky had got his claws into her—or, rather, she'd let him. She wasn't about to tell him he ought to leave the kid alone, though. She couldn't hack it if he turned his anger on her instead.

Chapter Eight

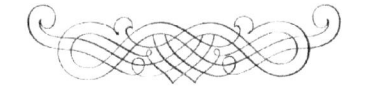

Amanda was still jittery from what had happened with the serial killer, Norman Wagstaff. Despite having CCTV in and outside her house, it didn't give her any feelings of security. Her house was tainted now that Norman had been inside it without her knowledge. She couldn't get her mind off what he might have done while he was there. She'd thrown all of her bedding away in case he'd done something disgusting, and the painting he'd stuck a mini camera to, she'd taken it down the tip. She actually wanted to empty the whole house, scrub the walls, repaint them and start again, but it would be less hassle to move away. But wasn't that a bit excessive, to uproot herself when previously she'd been so happy here?

Emma had been a godsend, checking in and making sure she was okay, popping round a couple of evenings a week so Amanda didn't feel so alone. Norman was dead, he wasn't a threat to her anymore, but it was like his ghost still hung around, reminding her of what had happened. Still, Emma had phoned earlier and asked if she could come round again. She'd be bringing dinner from the chippy, and she'd sleep on the sofa.

An hour later, Amanda let her in. "Are you okay? You don't look very well."

Emma took her coat off and hung it on the newel post. She didn't seem in a hurry to answer the question as she then took off her boots and placed them side by side next to the front door.

She popped her handbag on the hook above. "I've got a few things I need to tell you."

Amanda frowned. "What kind of things?"

"They're pretty fucking bad to be honest. It was shit I did when I was younger. Come on, let's plate this up before it gets cold." Emma took the brown paper package of food into the kitchen.

Amanda followed and sat while her cousin dished up fish, chips, mushy peas, and a pot of gravy each. Emma sat, and it was clear whatever she had to say hadn't affected her appetite because she tucked in straight away. Maybe she was comfort eating.

Amanda ate for a bit, and then curiosity prompted her to ask, "Why do you need to talk about it now and not back then?"

"Because I was shit-scared back then of the repercussions. Ricky could be a right mardy bastard when he wanted."

"Ricky McIntyre?"

"Yeah."

"And you're not scared of him now?"

"Well, yes, I am."

Amanda took a moment to get to emotions under control. It had upset her when she'd found out Emma had lied about studying with some girl called Laura when she'd really been with Ricky.

"You're probably not going to want me sleeping here tonight once I've told you everything," Emma said.

Amanda scoffed. "There's nothing you could tell me that would make me turn my back on you, if that's what you're worried about."

And it was true. Emma and Amanda were only children, so they'd pretended they were sisters when they were little. The only thing Amanda would change about Emma was the way she used to go and tattle to her parents about things, then her parents would tell Amanda's and they'd both be interrogated. Or lectured. Hmm, she'd stopped doing that as a teen, though. Around the time she'd hung around with Ricky.

"Our mums and dads can't know," Emma said. "And I mean *seriously*, they cannot know. If you think the Norman shit was bad…"

Amanda's stomach rolled over. What the fucking hell was going on? "Just tell me, will you?"

While they continued to eat, Emma started her story. To begin with, it wasn't anything Amanda hadn't imagined had gone on. Emma and Ricky fucking about, making a nuisance of themselves. Then things had changed, and Ricky had begun stealing, daring Emma to do it, too. Amanda couldn't get her head around that because it didn't match the Emma she knew.

"So you were a completely different person with him?"

Emma nodded. "The amount of times we were in places where we shouldn't be. He broke in, and sometimes alarms went off and we had to leg it. I've climbed over walls and all sorts. It was addictive, like being naughty gave me such a rush, but once I got home I felt bad. Mum and Dad would be so upset if they knew what I used to be like."

"They don't need to know. Let them think you're Little Miss Perfect still." Amanda smiled to take the sting out of her jab. "So is that it? Is that all you did?"

Emma took a deep breath and folded the edges of her chip paper over her leftover food and scrunched it into a ball. She got up and put it in the bin, then took wine out of the fridge and poured two glasses.

"So it's like that, is it?" Amanda asked.

"Just a bit." Emma sat and put her face in her hands. "I can't even look at you for this one."

"Just tell me, for fuck's sake."

"I was there when Ricky killed someone."

Amanda's whole body turned cold, and she stared at her cousin, who still had her face covered. What the fuck has she just heard? *Keep calm. She doesn't need me freaking out on her.* "What?"

The story unfolded quickly then, and Amanda lost her appetite. She put her food in the bin and returned to the table to sip her wine while Emma gave her the bare bones. Amanda felt sick. She remembered that lad dying and the police having no leads until someone had come forward. It had been in the local paper and online, and Emma had cried a lot, saying she'd had a bad period, but now it made sense, all of it.

"So that's why they moved to Wales," Amanda said.

"And now they're back. They were in the pub today. The men anyway."

"Is that the first time you've seen him since…"

"No. I didn't tell you about this last month because of what you had going on. Me being here with you during that time helped me take my mind off my own shit, but I'd been getting anonymous messages over Facebook. I knew it was Ricky because of what was said, and in the end I went to the police and got a restraining order. He got a slap on the wrist, they told him not to contact me again, and that was the end of it. Or so I thought. He then turned up in the pub yard one night when I went out for my break. He was just standing there in the dark, smoking."

"Fucking creep. You must have shit yourself."

"Yes, but I wasn't going to tell him that. He let me know it was him, and I told him he shouldn't be there, and he said something about what he should and shouldn't do had always been a problem."

"Do you think he was referring to the murder?"

"Probably. I reconfirmed I wouldn't say anything, and he brought up the restraining order. I said I thought it would have made him stay away, and he was all smug and told me there was no proof he'd been anywhere near me. I got cocky and said I could be recording him on my phone."

"Which was what you did with the murder. And probably why he's come back to bug you. He wants the footage."

"Yeah. Anyway, I told him to leave me alone and move on, and he said he couldn't because I know his secret. I reminded him I could get in the shit for keeping it to myself and I said for him to just walk away and we'll pretend we didn't know each other."

"What did he say to that?"

"He doesn't think he can do that."

"Fucking hell, man, that sounds really creepy."

"Which is why I was a bit unnerved because he came into the pub today. I spoke to him again, and I think he understands that I'm not going to be doing anything with the information I've got. They're probably going to make the Suits their local, so I'm moving. I'll ask if I can work at the Noodle instead. I can't bear to see him every day when I'm at work. Gordon's all right, he was so much younger than us when they had to leave for Wales, but Mr McIntyre… I kind of felt there was a threat there today. He was pleasant enough, but I don't know, something about what he said got under my skin. I'm worried they've come back for a reason."

Amanda's stomach churned. "What, to shut you up?"

Emma shrugged as if she wasn't bothered, but it was obvious she was crapping herself. "It's plausible."

"Why now, after so many years? It doesn't make sense. As far as I remember, the police thought it had been a random murder, something to do with the homeless community, and they weren't looking for anyone like you or Ricky. Have they found something out? Do they know that the police have opened the case again or what?" A light bulb went off in her head. "Shall we ring Colin?"

"Without telling the twins first? I don't think so. And anyway, if we ring Colin then he'll probably tell them what was said."

"What, all we want to know is whether the case got opened again."

"No, let's leave it. We'll have a Google later and see if anything new comes up."

"So what's the point in you telling me? Why bother if you're not going to get something done about Ricky?"

"Because I needed someone to know just in case."

"In case what? He does something to you? Him and his dad and brother attack you one night, is that what you're saying?"

"I just needed someone to know what I've done."

"I get that, but I honestly think letting Ricky walk around free is the wrong thing to do."

"But how do I get him either arrested or picked up by the twins without revealing my part in it? Without him revealing it, which he will. He's not going to go down on his own, he'll take me with him. I'd have to kill him myself to get rid of him." Emma snorted. "And that isn't going to happen."

"You could pretend you weren't there."

"But the police might have evidence I was."

"The twins, though. They'd believe you if you said Ricky had told you about the murder and you kept it a secret. They have no reason to think you were lying. Even if Ricky opened his mouth and said you were there you could deny it. They'd get rid of him for you, and that would be the end of it."

"It wouldn't, though, because there's Gordon and Mr and Mrs McIntyre, so that's four people who need to disappear. Could I have that on my conscience?"

"You said when you spoke to Ricky earlier on today he was open to having contact with you. Don't you think that's weird, considering the circumstances? Wouldn't you have thought he'd want to forget all this and move on as if you didn't know each other? What I'd be asking myself is *why* he wants to maintain contact. He was a sneaky little shit when we were younger, and I wouldn't put it past him to get all pally-pally with you, only to turn on you later down the line. What if they've come back to finish you off?"

"Fucking hell, Amanda! Did you have to scare me like that?"

"Yes. We have to look at all angles. You'll have to stay here with me until you get a new place. He turned up at your flat and now your work. I'm sorry, but that's sending a message, don't you think? Look how unhinged Norman was underneath it all. We already know Ricky has a bad side to him, so it isn't unreasonable to think their return to London has got something to do with you."

"They've been here a while, so why is he showing his hand now? Maybe *I'm* better off leaving London."

"Why should you be driven out when it's them with the problem?"

"I saw a murder and should have told the police. Even when it was in the papers and everyone was talking about it, I still kept my mouth shut."

"Because you were scared."

"Would the court see it that way, though?"

Amanda wasn't sure. Emma could get a sympathetic jury who understood that a teenager had been too frightened to open her mouth and had kept the horrors of a murder to herself for years, but what if the twelve people in charge of deciding the rest of her life were hard-nosed bastards who felt she was as much a delinquent as Ricky? What if they gave her a life sentence? It didn't seem fair.

"The only people we can turn to in this are the twins," Amanda said. "Yes, you're going to have to confess that you lied to them and said there weren't secrets in your past, but when you think about the gravity of the situation, what happened back then and what could happen now, don't you think it's better that they're informed so they can get rid of Ricky and his family?"

"That's four people you're talking about 'getting rid of'. It's just a mum and dad who wanted to protect their son, and I expect his brother is the same. They can't help this situation any more than I can."

"Listen to me." Amanda took a gulp of her wine, then leaned forward. "People like Norman and Ricky, who get off on scaring people, I've got no time or sympathy for them. If it means having you in my life and I'd get away with it, I'd kill Ricky ten times over. I mean, what is he even doing these days? I bet you any money he's robbing and pratting around as if he's still fifteen. People like him will never grow up. I couldn't give a shit if he's disappeared by the twins."

"They couldn't just disappear him, though, could they, without there being repercussions for me. The McIntyres are going to come straight to my door and ask me if I had anything to do with it. So it's like I said. George and Greg will get rid of all four of them rather than leave any loose ends. I just want Ricky dealt with. I don't want anyone else on my conscience."

"What if you hand over the footage? I don't mean completely. Make a copy and hand over one of them. Tell him that's it, that's all you've got, and that's the end of this bullshit. See how he takes that. His reaction determines what we do next."

"As in…?"

"Tell the twins, let them deal with it as they see fit."

Emma took a deep breath then let it out slowly. She swigged down the rest of her wine. "They must live on the same housing estate as the Suits if they were sizing it up as their new local. I can only hope they make a firm decision and come in again. I can talk to Ricky on a break and tell him I'll hand over the video. If they don't come in, then I'm reluctant to ask around to see if anyone knows where they live."

"I don't blame you, but this needs sorting either way. I don't like the idea of you moving from the flat and a job you love just because that little twat's come back. It sounds to me like he governed a lot of your life back then, so you should be fucked if you'll let him do it now."

"I won't. Why do you think I'm here? Why do you think I confessed? I needed help."

"Right. Then we'll do what I said. You speak to him, and we'll go from there."

Emma nodded, lost in thought, and Amanda delved into her own mind. The Norman crap had changed her. Ever since the twins had killed him, she'd lived with the knowledge that someone was dead because of her. Well, he was dead because of what he'd chosen to do, becoming a serial killer, but she had to grapple with the knowledge that she didn't care that he'd been murdered. She'd just wanted him gone. She'd wanted to feel safe again, and she didn't.

If she could dive into helping Emma with her problem, it would take her mind off her own. Wasn't that what Emma had done, too? And if at anytime she felt Emma was in danger and Emma didn't agree, Amanda would have no qualms about visiting the twins behind her back. As far as Emma would be concerned, Ricky just happened to have vanished. She didn't need to know George and Greg were involved. Amanda had become their eyes and ears for this street, and even though she'd be going against a member of her family, it was important to her that Ricky didn't get his hands on Emma. She couldn't shake the feeling that the whole McIntyre family was in on this, that they'd agreed to return to London to shut Emma up. And that sounded ridiculous now she thought about it. A family of four returning for one person when that person had never breathed a word about the murder until now.

Whatever, Amanda wasn't prepared to take any chances. The second this looked like it was going to shit, she was going to do something about it.

Chapter Nine

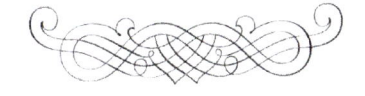

Ricky had gone back to the Suits and joined up with his dad and brother who were off their faces. He persuaded them to go for a little walk before they went home. The route he chose went down by the river, and at the bench where he'd sat with Mum earlier, he climbed on the low brick wall. If he leaned far enough against the railing, he'd topple over and into the water. Gordon got up there with him, to Ricky's right, and Dad, never one to be left out, got up on the left. Exactly as Ricky had known he would.

"Tell me about Karla from the Pigeon," Ricky said.

"Don't know who you're on about." Dad gripped the top bar of the railing.

"Fucking hell," Gordon muttered.

Ricky ignored him. "Come on, Dad. Tell us why you've been shagging some old slag when you've got Mum at home."

Dad huffed. "You're seriously barking up the wrong tree. Where did you go when you left the pub earlier?"

"I went and met Mum from work and walked her home. I got to thinking about how she hates London now, how she came back because of you, gave up everything she'd worked for in Wales because you'd said so, and what do you do? You take some bitch you met from work into a seedy room in the Pigeon and you fuck her like our mum doesn't mean anything. But then you've acted like that for years, haven't you? You probably think I never noticed. A quick squeeze of the wrist here. A slap of the face there. A hand around her throat and a thump to the stomach. Threats. Filthy looks. I saw it and heard it."

For whatever reason Dad imagined it was a good idea, he turned around on the wall and sat on the top bar. He wobbled, unsteady, and righted himself with what seemed great effort.

"Err, you'd best get down, Dad, you're going to fall off," Gordon warned, leaning forward so he could see Dad around Ricky.

That's the idea.

"She's going to go back to Wales, you know," Ricky said. "She's going to ask Gordon if he wants to go with her. I mean, he hated it when he first got there, but it ended up being his home, the same as it was for her. Why should those two have left just because I wanted to come back to London? Why couldn't you have stayed there for their sake instead of insisting we all come back together? I'm an adult, I don't need my family to tag along, thanks very much. What did you think, that I can't be trusted and I'll go off and murder willy-nilly without you there? Well, you were in the same city as me last time and you couldn't stop that, so if I wanted to do it again, you wouldn't be able to prevent *that* either. And just so you know, I hate you for how you've made my mum feel."

Dad looked down at his knees and wobbled some more. There was no way Ricky could nudge him without Gordon seeing, so he was going to have to say something to make Dad raise his fist and completely lose his balance.

"You're a no-good waste of space, do you know that?"

Dad whipped his head round to stare at Ricky. "Don't you speak to me like that."

Ricky sidled along, pushing his side into Gordon's to make it clear he was moving away from their father; he cowered away slightly to give the impression he was afraid of him. Then the fist whipped up, and the momentum sent Dad backwards and down, his knees keeping him attached to the top rung. He smacked his head on the lowest one, and then his legs broke free. He hit the water, the splash creating a sickening sound that whooshed at the same time Gordon shouted, "Dad!"

"Fuck," Ricky said. "Fuck!" He bent over. "Has he come back up?"

"It's too dark to see. Shit, what are we going to do?"

"Stick your phone torch on."

Ricky did the same, and they flashed the beams downwards. There was nothing but a few bubbles, then the awful quiet lapping of the water against the wall, their harsh breathing, and a giggle in the direction they'd walked. Ricky glanced that way. Two drunk women weaved along, and one of them held up a beer bottle.

"You'll fall off there if you're not careful," she slurred.

"Not fucking funny," Gordon snapped. "Our dad's just done that."

"Oh. Shit. Then phone the police or something. Let me see."

She climbed up onto the wall where Dad had been, so drunk she dropped the bottle. Dad's body popped up, facedown, the bottle smacking into the back of his head where a gash gaped from when he'd hit it. Had Ricky got lucky? Had Dad gone unconscious and then drowned? He'd been under for long enough.

"Oh, bloody hell," the girl said. "He really did fall in. I feel sick." She clambered down and tottered away, bending over to vomit on the pavement, her friend rubbing her back.

Gordon phoned for an ambulance. Ricky placed his mobile on the wall and jumped into the water to make a show of saving the man he despised. He didn't want to save him, but he'd noted others in his peripheral, so he'd had to act. The cold water swallowed him whole, and he propelled downwards, doing nothing with his arms to stop the momentum. The longer he faffed about before he popped back up, the better it would be. He eventually slowed, and the lack of air in his lungs sent him upwards whether he like it or not. He breached the surface, glancing around for Dad, and found that he was a few metres away from him. He swam his way, took hold of him and turned him onto his back, then checked for a pulse.

There wasn't one.

"He's dead," he shouted. "Fucking hell, he's dead. Someone help us, please, anyone!"

For some fucking stupid reason, Gordon jumped in. The splash jostled Ricky and their father, and he gripped Dad's coat to keep the body close. Gordon resurfaced and swam to the other side of him, and together, they trod water.

Ricky had never been so cold in all his life.

"What the fuck did you get in here for?" he said.

"You wanted help…"

"But there's nothing you can do. He's *dead*."

Gordon glanced up at the women who peered over at them. "I won't tell anyone, you argued," he whispered.

"Thank you, but I was nowhere near him when he fell."

"I know. But we'll keep it quiet anyway."

"What will we say?"

"That he was sitting backwards and fell, because that's what happened."

Ricky nodded, then he looked around for somewhere they could take the body out, but the wall along here was too tall.

Ricky's teeth chattered, the cold really setting in now. The blue lights of an ambulance flashed, and a minute or so later, a paramedic poked their head over the railing. There would be rope, there would probably be foil blankets, and there would be questions, but Ricky would get through it all.

Just like he had with the last murder.

Chapter Ten

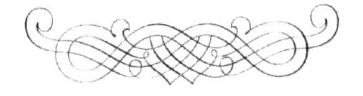

They'd been really bad tonight. Emma had lied to her mum and dad, saying she was staying at some girl's house. Laura, the name she'd chosen for her imaginary study buddy. She'd made up some bullshit that she was helping with Laura's little brother's birthday party, so it would be better if she had a sleepover. As Emma was such a goody two-shoes, or so

her mother thought, there had been no questions, and she'd stuffed a sleeping bag in her school rucksack along with food and a change of clothes, and off she went.

She met Ricky in the tree clearing, and they'd waited there until it had got really dark, then made their way to the building opposite the graveyard. Four homeless men lay on the pavement or were asleep sitting up against the wall, so Emma and Ricky darted down the alley on tiptoes and went inside the building, but then he dipped back outside and brought in half a pallet.

"What are you doing with that?" she asked.

"I'm going to break it up and burn it in one of the metal waste bins from the office."

"People will see the light through the window."

"Nah, I brought the tarpaulin, a hammer, and some nails."

It bothered her that he'd been so prepared, the word hammer *churning her stomach, but she didn't know why. It wasn't like he was going to use it on anyone, was it? Okay, maybe the mice, but she could cope with that. Sort of.*

"The smoke won't have anywhere to go, though, and we'll be breathing it in," she said.

"But we we'll be too cold otherwise."

"I thought that's why we bought the sleeping bags." Hers *was one Dad had when he was in the Territorial Army, so* she *wasn't going to freeze. He'd told her he'd slept outside in the snow and had been all snug.*

"Fair enough," Ricky said, grumpy.

She took her sleeping bag out and stepped inside it, doing it up, pulling the drawstring tight around her face, then hopping over to the wall so she could sit up in her cocoon. Ricky unzipped his like a quilt and draped it around his shoulders—he probably thought he was too manly to get in it like her. He was so weird sometimes.

"Who have you wanted to kill since I last saw you?" She'd picked his favourite subject so it put him in a better mood. She couldn't be doing with him having a cob on. It was too much hard work, and she was tired after a busy week at school.

"Spencer."

"Again?"

"Yeah."

"What did he do to set you off this time?"

Emma wasn't on the same timetable as Ricky at school, there were only a few instances their classes overlapped where he was coming out of one as she was going in, so she didn't always see his interactions with Spencer. The ones she had seen were uncomfortable and cruel, and she didn't see why it was necessary to be so nasty. Spencer used to smile all the time, he'd been so happy, and now he walked around with slumped shoulders, his eyes darting about as though he wanted to find Ricky before Ricky found him. She supposed it was like being a hunted animal and he knew he'd be a cornered one as soon as the corridors emptied out.

"He was in the lunch queue telling his mate that he was getting a new Xbox because his little cousin was having his. I mean, who the fuck gets a brand-new one if the one they've got is still okay? That family must have money coming out of their ears."

"That's a nice thing, isn't it? To give a little kid something like that."

"Must be nice to be in the position to be able to do it, yeah, but if I had a cousin, I wouldn't be handing over my Xbox, they could fucking go without."

Emma leaned her head back against the wall, glad of the cushioning of the sleeping bag between it and her hair. She didn't fancy spiders getting in it. She sighed. Several times now, Ricky had shown her that he didn't have a giving nature, that he was selfish and he considered his belongings his, and if anyone went anywhere near them, he'd flip his lid. Maybe that's what happened when you had a sibling. Emma wouldn't know, she was an only child and hadn't had to share her toys or whatever.

"I don't know who he thinks he is," Ricky grumbled. "Mother fucking Theresa?"

She'd have a go at trying to make him see but didn't hold out much hope. "Some people are just nice like that, though, aren't they."

"Why are you sticking up for him?"

"I'm not, I was just talking in general. Like some people are nicer than others, it's in their natures." It used to be in mine. *"Like nurses and stuff like that."*

"I get what you're saying."

"Maybe Spencer will end up being someone who helps others in his job."

"Do you even care what he ends up being?"

Even as 'nice Emma', she wouldn't have given Spencer's life a second thought, so it was no surprise that she said, "Err, no. I try not to think about what other people are doing when I need to concentrate on my own life."

"What are you gonna do?"

"I used to think I wanted to do something in finance, go to college and then uni, but since I met you, it's all gone a bit wrong."

He laughed. "So you're blaming me for not being strong enough to stick to your original goal? Fuck me, you sound like my dad. He always blames us lot for shit he should have dealt with himself."

While what he'd said had stung, he was right, in a way. It was Emma's choice whether she allowed Ricky to influence her, but what he didn't understand was he had a way about him where she felt she couldn't refuse. He was a gaslighter and a manipulator, she'd discovered that from reading a magazine article the other day, but he made her laugh and feel good about herself sometimes, and she felt special because he singled her out over everyone else. Was she so needy she was prepared to take whatever crumbs he threw at her when she actually deserved the whole cake?

That brought her up short, and she had the sudden urge to go home. It was dark out there and creepy in here, and she swore noises echoed in the building, like people walking with shuffling footsteps. She felt guilty for lying to her parents about where she'd gone. She'd abused their trust. Mum would be sitting at home now in front of the telly, imagining Emma giggling in her sleeping bag with Laura, who didn't even exist. She thought she was safe because Laura's parents were there to look out for her.

But if she went home now, Ricky would turn on her, she was sure of it. So instead, she took her phone out of her pocket and, keeping it inside the sleeping bag so Ricky couldn't see, she sent a message to Mum.

EMMA: NIGHT! XXX
MUM: NIGHT. LOVE YOU! XXX
EMMA: LOVE YOU, TOO.

"Who are you messaging?" Ricky asked, as if she wasn't even allowed to without his permission.

It got right on her nerves. "I don't have to tell you everything, you know."

"Who said you did?"

"It's the impression you give."

"Why have you gone all moody?"

"Says the boy who was moody before I was. Oh, but I forgot, it's okay for you but not for me." She really ought to keep her mouth shut.

"Bloody hell, what's up with you?"

"My period's due." It wasn't, but she'd lied so if she needed to leave, she had an excuse that she'd come on and hadn't bought any sanitary towels with her.

"Aren't you going to say sorry?" he said.

Here we go… *"What for?"*

"Saying shit to me."

"I'm not going to say sorry for making an observation. Can I tell you something without you biting my head off?"

"Go on then."

113

"You know you hate your dad, right?"

"Yeah..."

"And you told me you never want to be like him?"

"Yeah..."

"Sometimes you are like him."

"How do you know?"

"Because you told me the stuff he says to your mum. You've got the same sort of way about you with me."

"I didn't realise I was doing that."

"Well, you do." She glanced over at him to gauge his mood from his expression. It seemed safe enough to continue. *"So aren't you going to say sorry?"*

"I won't apologise for making an observation."

She gaped at him, but then he cracked up laughing. She laughed with him, because really, it was best to go along with it. She hadn't liked the darkness that seemed to float out of him when she'd tried to make him see how he made her feel. If she was going to have any kind of romantic relationship with him, which she doubted because he'd never made a move on her, then she'd have to give serious consideration to how he treated her, to how he clearly saw women, yet he banged on about his dad being awful with his mum so often she'd have thought Ricky would try his best not to mimic him.

"I'm going to kill Spencer one day," he said.

And here they were, back to a safer topic, even though discussing murder shouldn't be safe at all.

"How would you do it?" she asked.

"I'd use a knife. Stab the shit out of him."

"What about all the blood, though?"

"Okay then, I'd only need to stab him once because I'd pick the right place, and I'd have gloves on so wouldn't get any blood on me."

"Where's the right place?"

"Dunno. I'd have to look it up."

"If you look it up, you've left a trail that could lead to you."

"I'll use one of those internet cafés."

"They've probably got cameras, so the police would know you'd gone there."

"But the police wouldn't be looking for me, would they."

"Why not? You'd be a prime suspect because you bully Spencer, loads of people know that."

"So I'd ask someone where the best place to do it was."

"They could remember you asking because it would be on the news that Spencer was stabbed there."

"Never mind about working in finance, you should become a copper."

"I'm just playing devil's advocate."

"What's that?"

She couldn't be bothered to explain it in depth so said, "Pointing out pitfalls. You've got to cover your arse if you're going to kill someone. But this is all hypothetical anyway."

"Is it?"

"It had bloody better be, as even though we talk about it a lot, there's no way I'd actually kill someone, I've told you that before."

He cleared his throat. "It doesn't have to be you. I could do it on my own."

"Very funny."

"Who said I'm joking?"

"Pack it in now. Anyway, we've already said before that if you killed anyone, it would be your dad because you could make out it was self-defence and then you'd get away with it, get community service. You'd just have to walk around town picking up litter and shit instead of going to prison."

"Fuck off!"

"It's better than going in the nick, isn't it?"

"Hmm."

They didn't talk for a while, and Emma closed her eyes, tucking her face beneath the front of the sleeping bag to warm it. She still wanted to go home, her coccyx bone hurt from sitting on the hard floor, and while she was toasty enough now, not being in her own bed had her wanting it all the more.

"I can't get to sleep," he said.

"Me neither."

"Fuck this shit. I'm going home."

Panic reared up inside Emma. "But what about me?"

"What about you? You could go home, too."

"But I'm meant to be at Laura's. I told you I was saying that."

"So? Say you fell out with her and her dad dropped you off."

"No. They might want to speak to Laura's parents, ask me for her phone number, and I can't risk that. It'll come out that I've been lying and they'll ground me."

He got up and walked to the door in his sleeping bag cape. "I'll see you tomorrow then, yeah?"

"What? You're leaving me? On my own?"

"You could come and stay at my house if you want."

"Err, no, I don't want to be anywhere near your dad, thanks."

Ricky walked out, and she'd bet he expected her to get up, take the sleeping bag off, and run after him. But she'd show him. She'd bloody well stay here all night. She did take the bag off, though, the chill wrapping around her quickly, and she walked to the staff toilets. She went inside one of the cubicles, locked herself in, and put the sleeping bag back on. She sat with her back against the door. This was as safe as she was going to get here, and while she acknowledged she was being stubborn and bloody stupid, she couldn't bring herself to go home.

Every creak and groan of the old building settling for the night had her either jumping or crying out. Eventually, things quietened down, and she closed her eyes, too exhausted and bored to try and stay awake. It was then the doubts started. Ricky didn't care for her if he could just leave her like this. It was his idea to stay out all night, and he'd abandoned her without a second thought. She remembered the sweets, crisps, and can of Coke she'd put in her backpack for when they had their planned midnight snack. She'd have it in the morning for breakfast, and she'd also have a strong word with herself in the light of day. It was time to distance herself from Ricky. She just didn't know how she was going to do it.

Chapter Eleven

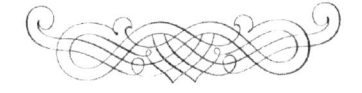

Meryl couldn't believe what the hell had happened. The knock on the door hadn't overly bothered her, despite it being late, because she'd expected her husband and sons to roll in. She had, however, told them to use a key. When she'd opened the door to find two police officers standing there, one of them with a high-vis jacket on, she'd suspected the worst. Her mind had gone straight to Clare Donaldson and that she'd arranged for thugs to beat the shit out of Ricky, but it hadn't been that.

She sat on her favourite armchair beside the fire, wishing it was the wood-burning stove in Wales. But it wasn't, it was a fan effort disguised to look like a real fire, complete with wavering flames behind a glass panel. The police officers sat opposite her. One of them had made everybody tea after Meryl had been given the news, and she hadn't said a word, not yet. She didn't trust herself. Verne was gone, at last, but Ricky and Gordon were not, and that was all she cared about.

"Do you feel ready to talk now, Mrs McIntyre?" PC Charlotte Smith asked.

The other one—Francis, Meryl thought he'd said his name was—smiled at her in sympathy. "We realise it's been a bit of a shock, but we have to ask some questions."

She nodded. Drank some tea. "Okay."

"Where have you been today?" Francis asked.

And Meryl laughed, she couldn't help it. "My husband falls off a wall in front of my poor boys, an accident, and you're asking where I was?

Here, or rather, I was next door until around half past eleven. I don't know the neighbour very well, just to say hello to, but I had a headache so I nipped round to ask if she had any tablets. She asked me in for a cuppa, and we got chatting. The time got away from me."

"And before that?"

She didn't know whether they were going to try and trip her up. She had the strong feeling that Ricky had engineered tonight's finale, and as she hadn't spoken to him since he'd walked her home, she had no clue what she was supposed to say. So she was going to have to go with the truth but add a little lie onto the end of it.

"My son, Ricky, left his father and brother in the pub to come and meet me from work and walk me home. We went along the river on the way and we sat on our favourite bench." *Favourite bench, my arse.* It was just a bench, a fucking shitty wooden bench, nothing more.

"Someone said they'd seen Ricky at the bench with a woman earlier this evening, so that must have been you."

"Of course it must, I've just said it was."

"Why is it a favourite?"

"It's somewhere we used to go when we lived here before we moved to Wales."

"Why did you move to Wales?"

"For my job. Why is that relevant to my husband being drunk and falling off a railing?" She sighed. "Can you see how pointless this sounds to me? I'm sitting here trying to process the fact that the man I was married to for decades has gone, and you're asking me why a bench is a favourite and why we went to Wales? Who gives a fucking shit? Do you? *Really*?"

Charlotte smiled. "Sorry, but we have to establish an alibi."

"For an accident? You said yourself when you came in it was an accident."

"Thank you for your time, Mrs McIntyre," Francis said. "Do you think your next-door neighbour would mind if you went back round or she came to sit with you? It's probably best you're not on your own at this time. Your sons are currently giving their statements along with other witnesses."

Meryl's stomach rolled over. "Thank God someone else saw it." Who the fuck was it? Would it cause problems for Ricky?

"There was a man and his girlfriend sitting on the next bench along."

Meryl calculated how far that was and whether anything that was said between her husband and sons could have been overheard. "Right."

"They saw your husband fall. He lost his balance."

"So asking me for an alibi *was* pointless." Meryl shook her head. "I'd like to be left alone now, please. I don't need anybody to sit with me. I shall wait up for my boys to get home."

She stood and chivvied them out so she could sit with her thoughts and get them straight before Ricky and Gordon arrived. She had questions she needed to ask herself. Why was she okay with the fact that Verne was dead and their son had most likely engineered his death? Was there something wrong with Ricky that he'd now killed twice? Last time he'd been creepily calm. Was he the same this time? Did he need to see someone to establish whether he had a mental health problem? But how could that happen without him admitting he was a killer? There were so many more swirling around her head, things she needed answers to, but she wouldn't be asking them in front of Gordon. Not unless he'd been in on killing his father, which she doubted.

She returned to her armchair, placed a throw blanket over her legs, and leaned her head back. She closed her eyes to imagine what the officers had described to her. Verne hitting his head, which seemed to have knocked him unconscious. Verne going beneath the water and staying there for some time. Ricky and Gordon hadn't been able to estimate how long, but both had said it had felt like forever before their father had popped back up. Two women coming along drunk, their night ruined by the death of a man who'd controlled Meryl all of their married life. It was hard to imagine herself free now, that he'd never tell her off again or hurt her.

She'd phone Joan in the morning.

Chapter Twelve

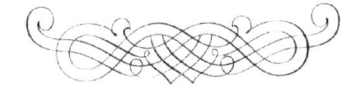

Daylight pierced through a chink in Amanda's living room curtains, and Emma squinted at the brightness. Her phone alarm was going off, the tune irritatingly jolly, and she reached down to the floor to pick up her mobile and silence the bloody thing. Without it screeching she could now wake up calmly, although her reason for being here popped up in her mind, bringing with it a sense of panic. Ricky wanting to maintain contact when there was absolutely no reason to do so. She tried to remember what she and Amanda had discussed last night, what they'd decided the best course of action was.

Oh yes, she was going to meet with Ricky to hand over the footage. Amanda had strongly suggested it be done in public. Emma wasn't to be alone with him. She was going to have to wait until he came back into the Suits. Would Kenny have kept his phone number when Ricky had asked about a job? She could have a root around in the office as it was Kenny and Liz's day off today, and Emma was doing a double managerial shift. She could get hold of Ricky and arrange for him to come into the pub. She could pass him the old phone that she'd recorded the murder on by hiding it underneath a packet of crisps or something. She'd wiped it of everything else, and if she handed the whole thing over it would make it look more authentic, wouldn't it, that he had the actual device. He might well say she could have forwarded the file to herself, which she had, to three different email addresses, but she'd swear blind she hadn't. And she'd just have to hope he believed her.

She got up and folded her bedding, placing it on the end of the sofa, ready to take up to Amanda's wardrobe before she left for work. She found her cousin in the kitchen making toast, the scent of coffee strong.

"Morning," Amanda said. "I've got to get to work early today because I've got to train up a new assistant."

Emma nodded. Amanda owned a clothing boutique and had struggled to find a replacement for Emma who had left, bored out of her mind serving rich women and needing a new direction in her career. She hadn't looked back since she'd started work at the Suits, although she'd had a day or so of working in the boutique in January so Amanda wasn't alone when Norman was still out there, the bloody danger to society that he was.

"I've got to be in for eight," Emma said. "It's Kenny and Liz's day off. They're going out somewhere, so I won't be back until late."

"Double shift for you then."

"Unfortunately, yes, but it gives me a chance to find Ricky's number and get hold of him. I need to nip home between shifts and get the mobile first, though."

"If this doesn't work and he still bugs you to keep in contact, then we'll move forward with the other plan."

Emma nodded, although the plan Amanda had come up with didn't sit well with her. It frightened her to death, to be quite honest. Cornering Ricky in the pub yard and tying him up, stuffing a cloth in his mouth, and then getting the twins to come and collect him. What the hell?

The toaster popped, and Amanda put the slices on a plate and passed it to Emma who spread butter and then Nutella on top. She sipped the coffee Amanda made for her, and they ate in silence. With breakfast over and the things cleared away in the dishwasher, Emma opened the Facebook app while Amanda was having a shower. Her newsfeed was full of utter shite lately, and for some reason it kept throwing up the local Facebook page, where people's main gripes were about fireworks upsetting their pets and a certain delivery company dropping parcels off to the wrong houses. Today's main event was different, though.

Just a warning. Part of the river's cordoned off and has been since last night. Some bloke fell backwards off the railing and drowned. He was called Verne McIntyre. Anyone know him?

MrsDoubtingThomas: I heard he was pissed as a fart.

> *John Simmons: dossnt matter whether you pissed or not it still a tragedy.*

MrsDoubtingThomas: Dossnt? What in the council estate language is that?

> *John Simmons: F U.*

Felicity B: Sending condolences. Must be awful for the fam.

> *Clare: I know who he is. His son killed mine.*

John Simmons: wot the F R U on about?

> *Clare: You'll see.*

> *John Simmons: U carn't just go round accusing ppl.*

> *Clare: Watch me.*

> *Jane Grace: Sorry to hear this news.*

> *John Simmons: just looked at your profile, Clare. you the woman where her lad got his back chooped up.*

> *MrsDoubtingThomas: Chooped? I worry for you, I really do.*

> *John Simmons: Y don't U go and do one, you old bitch.*

Emma closed the thread and moved over to Google to put in a search. A news article came up detailing the incident, mentioning that Ricky and Gordon had also been there, but Mrs McIntyre was round at a neighbour's house. Emma wasn't sure why that was relevant if a man, who had been out all day with his sons, had been drunk and fell backwards after losing his balance.

Did this change things? She couldn't be so cruel as to get hold of Ricky today, not now his father had died. It would be disrespectful and cruel of her, but she'd bet Amanda would tell her to still go ahead with it. But Ricky wasn't going to be in any mood to pop into the pub and collect the footage, not when he had his mum to deal with, plus his and his brother's grief.

She returned to the Facebook page and brought the post up, then made her way upstairs. At the top, she paused as Amanda came out of the bathroom. Emma handed over her phone.

"Before you read it, I'm telling you now, I am not getting hold of him about that footage, not today." Emma went into Amanda's bedroom and collected her clean clothes out of her overnight bag. She returned to the landing to take a towel out of the airing cupboard.

"Bloody hell," Amanda said. "At least there's some justice then. That Verne bastard was the one who threatened you, wasn't he."

"Yes."

"One down, three to go." Amanda handed the phone back and breezed into her bedroom. "Someone up there is looking out for you, missy.

Maybe if you wait long enough the other three will be dead somehow, too."

"The only way they'll be dead is if you go to the twins behind my back. I'm not stupid, Amanda. I know you're capable of it. But don't, okay?"

Amanda didn't reply, so Emma went into the bathroom, hoping the hot water would blast away the chill that had set up inside her. She washed her hair and closed her eyes, leaning her head back to rinse out the bubbles. She told herself it was going to be okay, that she could live in the same vicinity as Ricky, she could even see him every day if he popped into the pub, and there was no need for her to run. The problem was, the need to disappear was so strong she didn't think she was going to be able to ignore it.

She would speak to the twins, but it wouldn't be about Ricky. She was going to ask to rent one of their flats and if she could transfer to the Noodle.

George and Greg came into the Suits and ordered a fry-up and refillable coffee. Emma had asked them not to come in until she'd messaged them to let them know Kenny and Liz had left the building—the less questions from them, the better. She sat with the twins in the staffroom, having let Jackie, the other staff member on shift this morning, know that she had a few things to discuss and it needed to be done in private. She'd made out she was getting harassed by a customer and she needed the twins to sort him out.

"So what's the problem? Greg asked.

A massive urge to blurt the truth came over her, but she kept it inside. "I'm probably going to come across as an ungrateful cow because you've given me this job and whatever, but is there any chance I could move over to the Noodle? I'm asking because I need to be on the other side of the estate."

"Any particular reason?" George asked.

"I'd rather not say. And could I rent one of your flats over there an' all?"

"Relocating like that is a big step," George said. "What's going on?"

She was going to have to sort of tell the truth. "Look, somebody I used to know has come back to London and he started coming into the Suits. Said he's going to make it his local. He asked if we could keep in contact, probably to meet up after work and shit like that, and I don't want to."

"Why not?"

"Because that part of my life is over and I don't want anything to do with him. If you must know, I was a little shit when I was a teenager, except hardly anybody knew about it. I kept it from my parents. I was a good girl at home, but outside of the house I was a bitch. I hung out with this kid, and he was an arsehole. We got on. We had a laugh. But I'm older now, I don't want him reminding me of all the crap we used to get up to. It's cringe, know what I mean?"

"Yeah." George stirred sweetener into his coffee. "You could use your words and try just telling him you don't want to hang out. Or is he the type to not take no for an answer?"

"I'd rather remove myself from the equation."

"And what if he walks into the Noodle? What then? Are you going to move pubs and flats again?"

It sounded stupid now he'd put it like that. She couldn't keep running all over London, because Ricky would find her eventually.

"We could have a word with him if you like," George said.

"No, it's okay, I'll just explain to him, and if he doesn't listen, *then* I'll get hold of you, all right?"

"How come he's only just turned up like a bad penny?" Greg asked.

"He moved away to Wales with his family, then came back."

George whipped his head round to look at his twin. They said something without words, and Emma frowned.

George faced her. "Is it the McIntyre family by any chance?"

Oh God, how did they know? "Yes. The dad died last night in an accident."

"Yeah, I saw that on my feed this morning," George said. "The men of the family have been getting on certain people's nerves since they popped back up in London. We'd already sent one of our men over to The Eagle to keep an eye on them because the dad and the youngest son, think his name's Gordon, were getting loud when they'd had a few. The other one, Ricky, he didn't drink as much and was quieter. So they're thinking of switching from The Eagle to the Suits, are they? That's interesting. If they relocate then I'll send Jimmy here to keep an eye out. That way you'll always feel safe at work, won't you."

It was a good enough solution for now. "Thanks, I appreciate it."

"If there's anything you're not telling us, now would probably be the best time to spill it," George said. "Regardless of whether you've told us there are no skeletons in your closet, I'm beginning to think there are, and they're rattling, aren't they? They're making a bit of noise that you can't ignore."

Emma looked down, her eyes hot with tears. "It's fine, I can handle it at the moment. I doubt very much I'm going to be bothered by any of them, not now the dad's dead."

Greg sighed. "I suppose we're going to have to go and offer a donation for the funeral, considering the death is all over social media and we'll look a right pair of cunts if we didn't give his wife our condolences."

Emma wasn't stupid, she knew they were going to use this opportunity to check the McIntyres out in closer quarters. They'd likely suss out Ricky and Gordon to assess which one of them Emma was wary of, and they'd be able to work it out by their ages which one she'd hung around with. Fucking hell, she wished she'd kept her mouth shut now. Or better, she wished she'd thought it through logically before she'd even got hold of them. It was so obvious now that wherever she moved to, Ricky would probably find her.

The twins left the staffroom as their breakfast was ready. Emma went back behind the bar, Jackie asking if everything was okay.

"Yeah, it's fine," Emma said. "Nothing to worry about. And don't go telling anybody, even Kenny and Liz, that the twins are dealing with someone for me."

"I wouldn't dream of it," Jackie said. "All I'm bothered about is whether you're all right, and you said you are so…"

As there wasn't anything else to say, Emma smiled and walked off to serve someone. All she could do now was get on with her day.

Chapter Thirteen

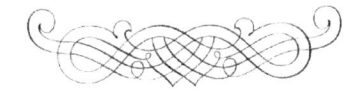

At some point before she dropped off, Emma had wedged herself in a front corner of the toilet cubicle, and the tight confines meant she'd felt a bit safer. She could pretend she was being hugged by her mother rather than two Formica-covered MDF walls. She woke in the same position, sweating. The sleeping bag really had done its job, but why was her heart

racing? Had she been woken up by something? She held her breath and listened, then folded her lips over her teeth and clamped them together at the tread of approaching footsteps. Whoever it was, their shoes crunched over loose bits of grit and God knows what else on the tiled floor. By the sound of them, the person was coming closer and closer. Bloody hell, what if it was a security guard? Or it could be Ricky. Maybe he cared after all, and he'd come to see if she was okay. If it wasn't for the fact she wasn't alone, she'd get her phone out to check if he'd even bothered to message her during the night.

Funny how that hadn't been the first thing she'd done when she'd opened her eyes. Usually she'd dive straight for her mobile to see if he'd sent anything. But then, she hadn't exactly had Ricky on her mind, had she? The footsteps were more important than anything he had to say.

"Who's there?" a man asked, his voice echoey.

Oh fuck, so she was going to get caught for trespassing. Her parents would find out because the police would be called and then she'd have to explain why she'd spent the night in a scabby toilet all on her own, at fifteen years old and something so out of character as far as they were concerned. But would that be such a bad thing, for them to know about this?

She'd be caught out in a lie and grounded, which would mean she wouldn't be able to see Ricky. When he messaged her, she could tell him she wasn't allowed to have anything to do with him anymore, that her mum and dad knew she'd been hanging around with him and not studying with a mate. It would take the onus off her. She wouldn't have to admit that while she'd enjoyed mucking about with him, she shouldn't keep doing it. Him talking about killing Spencer again was what had done it. It sounded like he'd actually meant it last night, it wasn't a joke or a fantasy anymore, and going from pretending to actually doing wasn't something she was prepared to engage in.

"I can see you at the base of the cubicle."

Shit. She remained quiet and didn't move. He must be on about the sleeping bag. The door didn't reach to the floor, the bottom edge was about five inches above it. If he wanted to, he could get down on his hands and knees and look under.

"We're not supposed to be in here," he said. "I saw you go in last night with that lad. I was going to come over then to say you had to get out, but I saw him leaving and I assumed you'd do the same, but I fell asleep so didn't check. We're paid by the owner to stay away, and if he knows you've been in here, he's going

to think it was one of us and stop giving us the money."

She felt guilty. "I'll leave as soon as I've had a wee an' that."

"Okay."

The footsteps started up again, and she listened until they didn't shuffle anymore—she'd actually counted how many there were and made sure they were fading, so she was sure he'd fucked off and hadn't just stood there walking on the spot to make her think he'd gone. A count to one hundred later, and she got her arms out of the sleeping bag and took her breakfast from her rucksack. She ate quickly, then stood and took the sleeping bag off completely, leaving it on the floor while she had a wee. God, it was cold. She used yesterday's knickers to wipe herself and then changed into her clean clothes. Outside the cubicle, she laid the sleeping bag on the floor and knelt to roll it up, then popped it into her rucksack, which she shrugged onto her back. She washed her hands and face at one of the sinks, drying her palms on her jacket.

How fucking insane was this, to be in an abandoned building getting ready to start her day. This time yesterday morning she'd never have dreamed this was where she'd be. The plan to stay here for the night hadn't arisen until lunchtime, which was a pest *because naturally, Mum had found it a bit sudden that plans had been made for Emma to go and stay at Laura's.*

She sighed and took her phone out to check the time. Just gone seven. She couldn't believe she'd slept all night, but then she remembered waking briefly a few times, uncomfortable, but forcing herself back to sleep. Groggy and aching, she tromped down the stairs and out of the building, not going home via the alley in case the homeless person who'd just spoken to her sat against the wall. She didn't want him to see her face in the daylight in case she and Ricky came back again another evening. Ricky had mentioned he wanted to clear the whole place of mice. He'd bought the BB gun she'd said about, and she felt so bad about putting the idea in his head.

She wasn't sure where to go so walked to town and went in McDonald's. She bought a coffee, getting warmed up at a table by the window. If she hung around until about nine, that wouldn't look a weird time for her to turn up at home on a Saturday morning. She could make out Laura was going out for the day with her brother and parents, maybe another birthday treat. No, it was best to keep it simple. If Mum asked, she'd say she didn't know where they were going.

Her phone pinged.

RICKY: DID YOU STAY THERE ALL NIGHT?

EMMA: YEP. SOME OF US AREN'T SCAREDY CATS.

RICKY: I WASN'T SCARED, I WAS BORED.

EMMA: WHATEVER.

RICKY: ARE YOU ARSEY WITH ME?

EMMA: YOU HAVE TO CARE TO BE ARSEY, AND I DON'T.

RICKY: YOU'RE LYING. I CAN TELL YOU'RE ANGRY.

EMMA: MORE LIKE BORED BECAUSE I'VE GOT TO WASTE SOME TIME BEFORE I CAN GO HOME.

RICKY: ARE YOU STILL AT THE BUILDING?

EMMA: NO, MCDONALD'S.

RICKY: WHICH ONE?

EMMA: IN TOWN.

He didn't answer, so that meant he was either going back to sleep or he'd come and sit with her for a bit. Maybe he wanted to have a word with her about her attitude. She had been rude to him over text, but fucking hell. If a girl had abandoned her last night, say it was Amanda, Emma would have been a damn sight ruder. She'd have told her exactly what she thought of her, yet she toned it down with Ricky because of any repercussions. She was also worried that, spiteful as he could sometimes be, he might anonymously let her parents know where she'd spent the night. She wouldn't put it past him at all.

So that was another reason to distance herself from him.

She finished her coffee and then got up. If he was coming here to see her then he'd be shit out of luck when he saw she wasn't there. It was still too early to go home, and none of the other shops were open, so she got on an idling bus that did a route around the Cardigan Estate. It would only cost her ninety-five pence to spend an hour in the warm. The bus would drop her back here, and she could go into a café for another coffee and a wee, then make her way home.

Emma sat upstairs at the front, her rucksack on the seat beside her, and it gave the impression that she was going to run away. Despite the fact she'd got herself in too deep with Ricky, she didn't feel as though she was drowning in anxiety enough to leg it. Although she would never want to, she'd tell her mum everything before she even thought of running to hide. Yes, she'd have to admit she'd done some bad things, that she'd lied through her teeth and had even stolen money out of Dad's wallet because Ricky had dared her to do it, but it was nothing that couldn't be fixed, given time. She'd rather make the break from him herself, though. Reaching out for help was the last resort.

As the bus pulled off, she caught sight of Ricky going into McDonald's. Maybe he did care then, just a little bit, or maybe he'd come to gloat that she was a right silly cow for staying at the building all alone. You never could tell with Ricky.

Chapter Fourteen

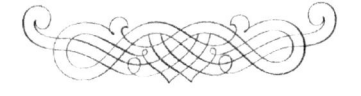

George and Greg quickly found the McIntyres' address and drew up outside their house which had several bunches of flowers lying on the front garden wall. George reckoned there would be a load of them down by the river, too, and as soon as the cordons were removed, some weirdos who'd been waiting all day would place them on the exact spot McIntyre had been prior to falling in. Undoubtedly a few would be thrown in the river. Christ, people were macabre.

"Wonder why Emma's uneasy regarding the McIntyre lad." Greg unclipped his seat belt.

"I wondered which one it was."

"If we go by age, it'll be Ricky, the quieter one."

"They say it's always the quiet ones you need to watch, don't they?"

"Is that a pop at me?"

George laughed.

They got out of the car, and he pocketed a wedge of cash in an envelope. It would be enough to cover an okay funeral. Three and a half grand wasn't to be sniffed at, and if the family did, then they could stuff it up their arses. George wasn't in any mood to pander to anyone, regardless of what had happened. The McIntyre men had been a pain in the arse for Jack and Fiona at The Eagle, so whether one of them was dead or not, there were black marks against them. The wife, though, there had been no reports about her, and it was her they'd come to see anyway, not her scrote kids.

At the house, George tapped on the glass in the front door and stood tall and straight. The door opened to reveal a thick-set, black-haired bloke of about twenty-two. His fat eyebrows met in the middle as the kid frowned, then his eyes widened and the caterpillars shot up.

"I imagine you've been expecting this," George said. "We've come here to pass on our condolences to your mother. I assume she's your mother."

"Yeah. I'm Gordon."

"Like the big engine." George had no fucking idea why he'd said that. "From *Thomas the Tank Engine*."

"Um, err, right… Come in." Gordon moved back.

Greg nudged George in the side, a clear admonishment for being such a dickhead. George entered the house and followed the sound of low voices coming through a doorway on his left. He stepped inside a modern living room and gave it a quick scan. Who George thought must be Ricky sat on a sofa beside an older woman who was undoubtedly his mother because they looked alike. The pair of them glanced over at him, and both seemed to jump at his size. George waited for Greg to join him, then George took one step forward and held out the envelope.

"We've come to pay our respects and to say sorry for your loss. I hope the money goes some way to helping with the funeral. We understand it can be a hard time financially. If there's anything else we can do to help, please let us know."

The woman smiled and took his offering, placing it on her lap. "Thank you, that's very kind. We were just wondering how we were going to afford everything, so this is a weight off. We're not going overboard, he wouldn't have wanted a fuss."

George, as ridiculous as he could sometimes be, couldn't resist a chance to make it clear that they were aware of this family's movements. "Where will you be having the wake, at The Eagle or the Suits?"

Ricky's eyes narrowed. "So the men at the bar in The Eagle were watching us and someone at the Suits was doing the same, were they? Any particular reason?"

"Your father and brother were making people uneasy with their loudness, their drunkenness. The Eagle is a nice quiet pub, no trouble is welcome there, and there was a worry that there would be. I gave you that explanation because of the circumstances and because I feel like being polite, but I will add that I don't have to explain jack shit to you about why there were people watching you and your family. You live on our Estate. By doing so, you agreed to abide by our rules. Should you and your brother decide to relocate to the Suits, then you'll be watched there by the man in the tartan. If you don't like it then you move on to a pub that we don't own, but seeing as those pubs pay us protection money, if you start up any hassle in them, please be aware we will be informed. We have zero tolerance for people who have a penchant for causing trouble."

"There'll be no trouble," the woman said. "None at all."

Chapter Fifteen

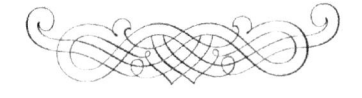

Meryl waited until Gordon had shown the twins out and returned to the living room before she spoke. "What the fucking hell have you three been up to in those pubs? What did I tell you before we came back to London? That we had to keep our heads down, mind our own business, but it doesn't sound like *you*, Gordon, or your father have been doing that."

"We were only having a laugh," Gordon said. "And you know what Dad gets like when he's drunk. Just a bit loud. The people in The Eagle are all the fuddy-duddy types who like peace and quiet, which is why we went to the Suits to see if that place was better."

"And is it?" she asked.

"Yeah, but that Emma works there."

Meryl tutted. "I've told you, she's no one to worry about. I'm more bothered about Clare Donaldson. Did you see what she said on that bloody Facebook page? What if the twins see the comment? They'll be back round here quick as a flash. We don't need them poking around."

"It'll be fine," Gordon said. "What happened to Dad was an accident. I suppose we ought to be grateful that this time we didn't have to pretend we didn't know anything about a body, making out we were surprised when word spread where he'd been found." He gave Ricky a filthy look.

"We've been over and over what happened in the past," Meryl said, "and we were all at home watching the telly with Emma, and that's what we'll stick to, no matter what, we all made a promise on that. And as for your snide comments towards your brother, Gordon, that's enough. If your father got himself so drunk that he couldn't keep his balance on a fucking railing, then he deserved to fall in that water."

"I can't believe you said that," Gordon said, his voice hushed.

"I said it because it's true. And he deserved to fall in because of the way he treated me. I've suffered at his hands for years, and now it's over, it's ended, and I can actually live the life I want. By *my* rules. I've already phoned Joan, and she's agreed I can stay in her spare room until I find somewhere in Wales. I start back at my old job next month. You two can continue to rent this place if you want, we'll get the estate agent to switch it to your names, but I'm telling you, London is evil, it isn't the place for me to see out my days, so I'm going back to where I feel most at home."

She wasn't about to tell them that a man waited for her there. A man she'd hated to leave, but she'd had no choice. She'd emotionally cheated, they hadn't gone anywhere near each other sexually. Christ, they hadn't even kissed. They'd worked together and spent their lunch times together, pouring their hearts out to one another about how unhappy they were with their spouses. So not only had she phoned her former employer and Joan, she'd also phoned Damien who'd left his missus soon after Meryl had waved goodbye to Wales because he couldn't hack being with his wife anymore.

Given time, her boys would accept a new man in her life, and if they didn't, that was tough. For too many years Meryl had lived by someone else's dictation, and it was about time she took the reins and steered her own horse, not the scabby donkey Verne had ridden in on.

Chapter Sixteen

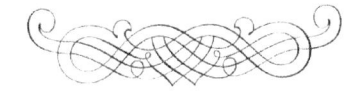

Ricky couldn't stand the suffocating atmosphere any longer. He understood Mum had every right to revel in her freedom, but he worried she'd slip up in public. If they could just get her through the funeral with her acting like a genuine grieving widow, then she could bugger off to Wales and never have to see any of the people around here again.

He left his brother and mother at home and walked to the Suits—there was no way he wanted to go to The Eagle, not now he knew they really weren't welcome there. He'd sensed it before, but to be basically told to fuck off… He supposed George had meant the same applied to the Suits, but now Ricky had discovered Emma worked there, he found he couldn't stay away.

He pushed open the main door and strode inside, clapping eyes on her straight away. He was going to continue this charade, pretending to be friends with her, and once she believed he meant her no harm, that was when he'd hurt her. He could tell by her face that she'd heard about Dad. She had that look where she was going to pass on meaningless condolences. He couldn't give two fucks that his dad was dead, just that he was gone and he couldn't upset Mum anymore.

He reached the bar and placed both hands down on it. "A Diet Coke, please, one of those refillable ones."

She frowned at him, as though it was anathema to not ask for a couple of shots of spirits to be put into his drink. He could very well do with some rum or vodka, but this was all part of the plan to make her think he'd changed, that he wasn't the alcohol-swilling teenager she once knew, the kid who drank it straight from a bottle nicked from his dad's drinks cabinet.

She poured the Coke and handed it over. "That one's on me."

He shook his head and produced his card. "I don't need your charity."

She sighed and held the card reader out to him, the beep loud between them. "I can at least say I'm sorry for your loss, though, which I am. Sorry for you, I mean."

"But not my dad."

"No."

"I don't blame you. The way he spoke to you… He spoke to my mum like it all the time behind closed doors. I can't say I'm going to miss him. I've hated him for years."

One night, when they'd got drunk on Mad Dog 20/20, he'd told her about the abuse towards Mum. Emma had hated Dad right along with Ricky, and they'd flung themselves back on the grass and stared at the stars while they'd plotted how they'd kill him. That was how they'd been as teenagers, plotting to kill anyone who pissed them off. He'd known Emma so well then, yet it was like he didn't know her at all anymore. Who she'd been perhaps no longer existed. The girl who'd seemed to have as much desire to commit murder as him had tucked herself away when his family had scuttled off to Wales. She'd probably buckled down, behaved like a normal human being, and these days liked to pretend she'd never had bad thoughts at all.

Maybe it was only him who still had them. Maybe teenage hormones made you think weird things and when they finally settled down, you weren't supposed to think them anymore. It was sobering to acknowledge she'd moved on and he'd stayed in the same headspace.

"How's your mum?" Emma asked.

Years ago, he'd have trusted her and told her the truth immediately. But these days? No, he wasn't going to reveal anything about his family that could be used against him. "She'll cope."

"I want to hand my phone over to you. The one I had back then."

He nodded, seeing a glimpse of the old Emma, the one he could trust. She must want this to end for him to have the recording. But he was going to have to double-check. "Handing the phone to me doesn't mean there aren't copies of the video file."

"But there aren't. I want this over with. You can destroy it, and then none of us have got to worry. I don't want you hanging around my arse any more than you want me threatening to give the phone to the police." She glanced across at a nearby customer who sat on a bar stool to check they weren't being listened to.

To be honest, if he left things as they were, this would bug him till the moment he snuffed it, wondering whether this or that day would be the one where she'd walk into a police station and reveal all, so it was better that he got rid of her for good, wasn't it?

"I'm working a double shift. But I've got an hour off at five," she said. "I can pop home and get the phone and give it to you in here at half past."

Had she said that to make it clear to him that she was due back behind the bar by six and that if she didn't arrive, somebody would notice? Did she suspect he had ulterior motives towards her and would follow her to get the phone? He supposed it wouldn't be surprising if she did, considering the way he'd hidden in the dark yard and likely scared her in January, but he'd still been angry then, he hadn't had a proper plan in place. And if he was being totally honest with himself, he'd missed her, and there was a part of him that wondered whether deep down, she still had those nuggets of nastiness inside her, whether they could still be the twosome they'd been when they were kids.

"That's fine by me," he said. "We'll meet out the back."

She flinched.

"Do you have a problem with that?" he asked.

"No." She smiled a liar's smile.

"And thanks, you know, for wanting to put this behind us."

"I always did, but *someone* decided to send me anonymous messages." She smiled again, probably to show him she hadn't meant it as a proper dig, but that she'd had to make the point all the same. "You could have just said a normal hello when you got back to London, and that would have been the end of it."

He realised that now. Yeah, he could definitely see it in her eyes that she wasn't lying this time. "Does it bother you at all, what happened?"

"This is something we ought to talk about in private." She jerked her head at the other customers down the bar. "But for now, I'll say sometimes. Bad dreams and things. I haven't slept too brilliantly since you've been back."

That had been a fair while, and it gave him a measure of satisfaction that he could affect someone as much as that. Or was it the murder that had affected her? Her part in it? What sentence she'd receive if it ever went to shit and they ended up in court. Because it would have to go to court. There was no way he was pleading guilty. There was no proof he'd even been there apart from that recording.

"Are you sure the only version is on that phone?" he asked.

"I wouldn't lie to you about something like that. It's too important to fuck about with."

He nodded in answer and as a 'bye for now', walking over to a small booth so it would give him the anonymity he needed. There were a couple of Dad's work mates in here who hadn't spotted him yet, and the last thing he wanted was them coming over and raising a glass to a father who had been a cock for the most part. All right, he'd been brilliant to agree to hide the murder, but he really had been a dickhead ever since, keep reminding everyone when they'd been in Wales why they were there. *And* who'd made them leave London. Ricky had been under no illusion that it was all his fault. Of course it was. He'd fucking killed someone and had never denied it to his family. He didn't need reminding of it because he played it over and over in his head at least once a day for entertainment purposes.

He took his phone out and browsed social media. Someone had put up a post about Dad on the local Facebook page, and while Ricky didn't particularly want to read it, he was going to have to gauge the mood and what people's perceptions were. The police had swallowed the story—after all, it had largely been the truth apart from not mentioning the argument—and neither Ricky nor Gordon were under suspicion, but still, people's theories gained traction at an alarming rate these days, and conspiracy theories were born from armchair detectives who didn't give a single fuck whether their words were damaging or not.

Did you see that the police are asking for witnesses to come forward about that bloke who drowned in the river last night? I heard it was an accident, so what do the coppers want CCTV for? Do they think the sons did it? I bet you the man was a right bastard and they bumped him off and made it look like he just fell.

Dave King: That's slander.

> *Janet Moss: I think you'll find that's libel because he wrote it.*

Dave King: Picky cow. You know what I meant.

> *Haters_Gonna_Hate: The grammar police are out again.*

Janet Moss: It's my favourite hobby.

> *Dave King: Weirdo.*

The rest of the replies were a mix of condolences and theories, but the original poster was the only one who'd got it right, apart from 'they' bumped him off when it should have been 'he'. Still, it was unnerving that Dad's death was being discussed as though it was murder, plus the OP was correct on the first part of his post, too. Why *did* the police want CCTV footage?

Fuck it, he was going to respond.

> *Ricky McIntyre: I'm one of the sons. Sorry to piss on your amateur detective party, but as the police have already told us we're not suspects, you're wasting your time in this discussion. I don't understand how someone can get pleasure from throwing rumours around when a whole family is grieving. Can you at least have some respect for my mum?*

> *Clare: Like you had respect for me when you killed my son?*

Ricky's stomach rolled over. She'd replied almost instantly, so what was she doing, stalking the page? What should he do, ignore her or respond? His silence could mean two things. One, that she didn't deserve a response because she was chatting shit, or two, he was guilty and didn't want to incriminate himself by answering her. He'd at least acknowledge she'd typed something.

> *Ricky McIntyre: I think you must have got me mixed up with someone else. I've never killed anybody. I'm sorry for your loss.*
>
> *Clare: So you say, but I know the truth.*
>
> *Ricky McIntyre: Sending hugs.*
>
> *Clare: You fucking sarcastic little prick.*

If he hadn't caused hassle with Emma, he could have gone to the police and told them about what Clare had written, but they probably weren't going to give him the time of day considering he had a restraining order on him. It had been brought up when they'd questioned him after the ambulance had taken Dad away and they'd gone to the station, but a second officer had changed the subject, likely thinking it wasn't exactly appropriate to bring something like that up when his father had only just died. Maybe he could persuade Emma to get the restraining order squashed. Or was that too soon?

He'd finished his Coke so went up to the refill machine and poured another. Emma glanced over, and he jerked his head to let her know he needed to speak to her.

"Everything all right?" she asked.

"I've been thinking. Is there any need for the restraining order? I'm breaking it by being in here, and you're supposed to have told the police I've come too close to you. I'm sorry I sent those messages and stood outside your flat, I was an absolute dick."

"I don't understand why you even did it. I mean, I get it, because you said you didn't want me to tell anyone what happened, but you know me, and you know I wouldn't have. It just seemed a waste of time, scaring me for something I didn't need to be scared for."

"I didn't know that, did I?"

"You must have because I never took the footage to the police all that time."

"Fair point. Truce?"

"Yeah. I'll speak to the police, okay?"

"Cheers."

He returned to the booth and Googled his father's death, finding a post on Reddit, more armchair detectives with nothing better to do than theorise. He thought about Gordon and how his temper was quick to flare if too many buttons were pushed. He was going to have to have a word with him and reiterate how important it was that the row with Dad was never mentioned, not even to Mum.

It was going to have to be their secret.

Chapter Seventeen

Ricky had decided it wasn't a good idea to go back to the building so soon after the homeless man had spoken to Emma. She wasn't going to complain about that because it meant the mice would get to live for a bit longer, oblivious to the fact that their murderer planned to pop them with little baby bullets or whatever the hell went in those guns. She reckoned

he'd probably ask her to shoot some, too, but she was going to do that thing she did where she said she preferred to watch. It got her out of doing so many things.

It was tiring to keep lying. It seemed she lied to everyone in her life now, including Ricky. Because she couldn't completely be herself with him, she had to watch what she said before she spoke in case it set him off. Her stomach churned sometimes when she wanted to bring something to his attention but worried about his reaction. If someone made you afraid like that, then they weren't anybody you should be anywhere near, but this stupid hold he had over her, or some kind of magnetism between them, kept drawing her back. She could have lied to him and said her parents had found out where she'd really been that night but she'd ended up falling back into this pattern of meeting up and fucking about.

It had to come to a natural end at some point, didn't it? She hadn't allowed herself to completely fall under whatever spell he'd woven, she could see he was an arsehole sometimes. Or a lot of the time. And she was well aware he wasn't normal in the head. Every so often, he said something really sinister, and she reckoned he knew she contemplated doing a runner.

How stupid that she didn't when she had a valid excuse right at her fingertips. What did that say about her that she didn't use that excuse? Why did she hate the way he spoke to her sometimes yet put herself through it every day after school and at weekends? It didn't make any sense. Maybe it was because meeting Ricky had shown her how boring her life had been before he'd come on the scene. Maybe the thought of going back to having evenings at home or spending them with Amanda was too tedious to imagine. She'd tried to persuade Amanda to come out with her, but she'd said it was boring walking around the streets doing nothing. And she'd had a point, because with Amanda there wouldn't be anything to do, but with Ricky there was. Amanda would never kick a street sign until it leaned over. She wouldn't shoot mice.

What the fucking hell have I got myself into?

Emma lay beside Ricky in the tree clearing, thoughts too swirly, her emotions chaotic. She wanted to get up and run, but that would look weird if she did that. Did it matter, though? Ricky often fucked off home when he felt like it, and she'd swear it was at times when he got overwhelmed and needed to distance himself from whatever he was doing or had done. So why couldn't she do the same? She could, but she felt like she couldn't. Ricky would have something to say about it, and explaining herself...God, she couldn't be bothered.

"What are you thinking about?" *she asked him and prayed he didn't say Spencer.*

"I heard my mum talking to one of the neighbours earlier."

"What about?"

"Fucking off. Taking me and Gordon with her and not telling Dad where we've gone."

Emma's stomach turned over with hope. Had fate just handed her an out? She had to fight off a massive smile. "That's not a bad thing, is it? At least you wouldn't have to see him picking on her anymore and she wouldn't have any bruises."

"I know, but it's Wales, and that's miles away. It means we'd have to go to new schools. Well, Gordon would because I'd be finished soon. We wouldn't know anyone."

That little reveal of insecurity surprised Emma, but she pretended he hadn't shown the chink in his armour by saying, "It's not like you hang around with anyone at school really, is it? You're mainly on your own, so if you went to college it'd be no different."

"I suppose so, but I still know people here. I could still stop and talk to them if I wanted to."

"Why Wales?"

"She's got a mate there called Joan who used to live in London. They worked with each other or something, I don't know. But what I do know is that she's even gone so far as to plan when we'll leave. I mean, she's going to wait until Dad's gone to work, then we'll quickly pack a suitcase, essentials only, she said, and we'll get on the train. She said Dad wouldn't think we'd ever go somewhere like that. He'd be more likely to imagine we'd stayed in the East End."

"It might be nice to start again. I think about doing that all the time."

Of course, he didn't realise she'd meant with regards to him. Ricky was the type of person who couldn't imagine somebody wouldn't want to hang around with him anymore. He was up his own arse like that, had a big ego. But was that true? He'd just been vulnerable, worried about having no friends… Christ, she couldn't work him out.

"Where would you go?" he asked.

"Probably abroad. Somewhere hot. It's always raining here, and it pisses me off. Everything's so grey."

"We do have sunny days, though."

"Few and far between. I prefer to see sun every day over clouds."

"I suppose I could kill my dad and that would mean we wouldn't have to move."

"Yeah, the self-defence angle like we talked about." She shouldn't be encouraging him to kill someone, but what if it went in her favour and self-defence wasn't considered? What if they thought it was premeditated murder because he was aware of his dad treating his mum like shit and he wanted it to stop? The jury might feel sorry for him, but he'd be put in the nick anyway, and then she wouldn't have to wean herself off him. She remembered telling him he'd get away with picking litter instead of going to prison. Bloody hell, she hoped that wasn't true.

Why don't I wean myself off now? Why don't I get up and go home like he does when he's had enough?

"Spain then," he said.

"The Caribbean. Mexico. Turkey even."

"Drinking cocktails by the pool."

"Pretending I was eighteen like Sasha and old enough to live by myself. Pretending I was strong and I didn't have to answer to anyone."

"Was that a dig at me?" he asked.

"If you took it as one, then yes. If you say it's a dig then it's a dig, isn't it? I couldn't possibly have meant something else, could I."

"Oh God, you've gone stroppy again."

"Teenage hormones."

"I only ever let you get away with giving me lip."

"What do you want me to do about that, pop champagne?"

She glanced at him to see if she'd gone too far, and he looked back at her. The silence stretched out for a moment, then he laughed his head off. He sobered quickly, though, frowning and staring at the sky.

"If my mum had bitten back at my dad like you do, then maybe he wouldn't ever have hit her because he'd have known she was too strong to put up with his crap."

"Are you saying I'm strong enough to put up with yours?"

"If you'd let yourself, yeah. You hold back most of the time, though, like my mum does. Kind of like you're picking your battles."

"To be honest, I can't be bothered to argue with you," she lied. *"I'm not walking on eggshells with you, because I refuse to be someone who does that. There's a difference between watching what I say and do because I'm worried about what your reaction will be, compared to sitting back and letting you get on with it because it's less hassle."*

"It could be dangerous, though. What's that saying? Give them an inch and they'll take a yard."

"So you were doing it on purpose then? What am I, some kind of experiment so you can understand the dynamics between your parents? Fucking charming." She tacked on a laugh to make out she didn't care.

"I don't know what *I was doing. I don't even know why I started hanging around with you."*

"That's the same for me. We're not exactly suited, are we?"

"We have proved that a nerd and a scally can have something in common, though."

"What's that then?"

"Planning murders."

"Err, no. We're not planning them, we're just talking about them. And there is no way *I would ever do one."*

"I know. You must wonder, though. I think about what it'd be like to put a knife in someone's body. What it would feel like slicing inside. I stabbed Mum's joint of pork the other day to get an idea, and I reckon doing it on a human being would be a lot harder."

"Why d'you say that?"

"Dunno."

He killed mice. He'd knifed a piece of pork.
Who the fuck was he?

Chapter Eighteen

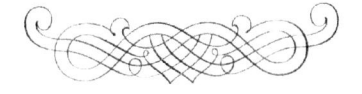

Emma left the pub via the back and rushed home to collect the old mobile. Five o'clock had come around so quickly, with Ricky staying in the pub all that time drinking Coke after Coke. She wasn't going to get hold of the police about the restraining order. She'd rather keep it in place, not trusting his efforts in trying to get her to believe everything was okay between them now. She knew what he was up to and she wasn't going to fall for it. She had to be on her guard when it came to him.

She recalled their many conversations, how they'd been obsessed with talking about murder, although she'd grown out of wanting to do that as soon as an actual murder had been committed in front of her. He wasn't supposed to go that far and really do it. She'd misjudged him. She'd thought he was the same as her, only wanting to play a game of pretend. Imagining killing their geography teacher who got on their nerves was completely different to killing for real. Imagining killing Spencer…

Their chats had clearly meant something different to Ricky.

She'd often looked back on her old self and wondered why she'd even had those conversations with him. Why had she even *wanted* to? Yes, she'd had a lot of angst going through her on the daily, hormones and whatever, but she'd had no reason to say such nasty things or to think them either. Mum and Dad would be horrified if they ever found out.

Which was one of the reasons why, in an ideal world, the twins could get rid of Ricky so Emma's shame would never come to light. But would they insist she told them what that shame was? And would she be punished for her part in everything? Unless she made out she'd been forced to video Ricky, forced to watch. The footage had proof of her gasping and crying. She'd sounded distraught, so she could get away with that little story, but would she be brave enough to maintain it if George and Greg insisted she confronted Ricky while they were there?

She didn't even know why she was thinking this.

She let herself into her flat and got down on her hands and knees, stretching an arm under her bed to pull out the box right at the back. It contained shit from her teenage years. A diary, a notebook, a few CDs and trinkets. The phone. She grabbed it, wiped her fingerprints off it using her woolly gloves, and stuffed it in her pocket. In the kitchen, she put a microwave curry in to heat. She scoffed a slice of bread and butter while she waited, then wolfed her dinner down in between blowing on it madly because it was too hot. At twenty past five, she headed back to the Suits and waited by the yard gate. She hadn't wanted to meet him alone, yet she'd gone back to bad habits and obeyed him.

Ricky appeared from around the corner and stood beside her, lighting a cigarette. "Hand it over then."

She took the phone from her pocket and switched it on. "There's nothing on there except the video. No messages between us, nothing."

"Why delete the messages but not the video?"

She shrugged. "I think it was more insurance against your dad. You know, if he ever got funny with me, then I could show him the video so he knew to leave me alone. But then you moved to Wales so…"

"…it wasn't needed."

"Yeah, and I made out to my mum and dad that I'd lost my phone so I could get a new one. I shoved this one under the bed and forgot about it."

"I shit myself when you didn't reply to my texts when we first got to Wales, but Mum said she'd spoken to you and said to cut contact completely. Is that true?"

She wasn't sure whether to lie or not. Mrs McIntyre hadn't said any such thing. "I can't remember."

"I did wonder whether she'd said that to me to make me feel better."

Emma wasn't going to respond to that. The farther she kept herself away from that rabbit hole the better. "Anyway, I'd best get inside so I can have a coffee and a sit down before I have to go back to work."

"Right. Well, thanks for this." He held the phone up, then put it in his pocket.

"I assume you're going back in the pub."

"No, I'd best go home and see if Mum's all right. I've been gone too long as it is."

She refrained from saying that he could have gone to see her at any point this afternoon but had chosen to sit in the booth. Best she didn't antagonise him.

They walked round the front together, and at the door, she watched him stride away in the dark, hands in pockets, and she wondered whether one of those hands gripped that phone. Did he believe her that it contained the only version of the video? He'd seemed to take her word for it, but who knew whether he'd mastered the art of hiding his expressions. He'd been good enough at it as a teenager, but he could be a pro now.

She waited for him to round the corner and then lit a cigarette. She didn't have to sit down, she'd used that as an excuse to get away from him. There was only so much of his presence she could take, and as he'd been in the pub for a few hours, she'd been being seriously on edge and needed to distance herself from him.

Maybe now he'd move on and leave her alone, even if he chose the Suits as his local. They didn't have to be pally-pally for her to serve him like any other customer, and some of the punters who came in got right on her last nerve and she couldn't stand them, yet she smiled and pretended everything was okay. She could do the same with Ricky. All she had to hope was that he didn't want to take this new, fragile friendship to the next level. Maybe he'd be too busy now, helping his mum get the funeral sorted. He wouldn't have the time to sit around in the background of her life.

She hoped.

Chapter Nineteen

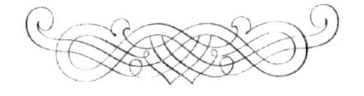

Gordon had convinced his mother to let him go back to Wales with her. He wasn't going to stay with Joan, he had a mate's sofa with his name on it. She'd queried why he wanted to go back when he'd kicked up such a fuss about leaving London in the first place, and he'd explained that returning to old friends who clearly hadn't missed him, nor did they give a shit about him now, well, he was better off with those he'd made in the village. That would mean Ricky had got his own way after all, living in London by himself.

Life without Dad was going to be weird. He and Gordon had fallen into a pattern since coming back to London. Working together, drinking together, Dad acting more like his buddy than his father, which had been nice. It was going to take Gordon a while to accept the dad he'd known wasn't who Verne McIntyre had really been. With Ricky out of the way this afternoon, Mum had opened up about her marriage, and at first Gordon had shaken his head. He hadn't believed the crap that came out of her mouth, but she'd shown him some recent bruises from just the other day where Dad had gripped her wrist.

Was that where Ricky got it from, that need for violence? He'd goaded Dad on those railings, and Gordon had got the sense that his brother had received the result he'd been trying to achieve — Dad falling and dying. Now Gordon knew about the systematic abuse Mum had suffered, he could understand Ricky getting rid of the bloke, but it had brought back questions from the past. Ricky had told the police last night that it had been an accident, and he'd said it in exactly the same way as he had with that kid who'd been murdered.

Was Ricky someone to worry about?

That was the reason Gordon had approached their mother about going back to Wales with her. He needed to distance himself from Ricky. He wished he could erase everything that had gone on, but unfortunately, it paraded around his head in hobnail boots—Ricky's decisions and actions were something they'd all lived with for such a long time, and Gordon was sick of it.

No more.

Chapter Twenty

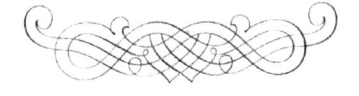

Ricky entered the house, quietly waiting in the hallway for a moment to assess his surroundings. The telly was on, the low murmurs of conversation giving him the hint it was a chat show. The scent of fish and chips lingered; maybe Gordon had been sent out to collect their dinner or, wonders would never cease, he'd suggested it himself. Ricky questioned whether his brother would have bothered getting him any, but of course he would, Mum would have reminded him to. She was good like that.

If she was in the living room with Gordon, then they weren't talking.

"Is that you love?" she called.

It was on the tip of his tongue to retort that it wouldn't be anyone else, what with Dad being dead, but that would be cruel, and besides, Gordon might have gone out and she'd thought he'd come back in. And anyway, Ricky needed to change his ways, his thoughts when in anyone's company, so they all thought he was a nice enough fella and no one to worry about, especially if the police came back to ask more questions about Dad's fall. Who knew whether they kept an eye on the social media posts.

"Yep. Something smells good," he said.

"Yours is on the side, still in the wrapper. Gordon's not long gone and got it, so it's probably still warm."

It didn't matter, there was always the microwave. "Thanks."

He took his shoes and coat off, putting them away, then went into the kitchen. He plated his food up and popped it on to heat for thirty seconds while he grabbed a Fanta from the fridge.

"Does anyone want a drink bringing in?"

Their responses of "no thanks" sounded subdued, and he dreaded what he was going to walk into when he went into the living room. He had to remind himself that it was okay for him, he only felt relief that Dad was gone, and even though Mum claimed earlier to hate him and she'd been devising ways to leave him, it still must hurt that her husband had died. But it was Gordon who needed worrying about. Him and Dad had been getting on like a house on fire since they'd come back to London—probably because none of Gordon's friends had wanted to know him, and Dad was the only person he had to hang around with because he wasn't Ricky's cup of tea. An uncharitable thought, but a true one.

He took his dinner and can into the living room and deliberately sat in Dad's favourite armchair. Mum glanced over from hers and raised her eyebrows at him but then switched her attention back to the telly. Gordon shook his head and puffed out air as though he thought Ricky now had the idea he was the head of the family.

"I've always sat in his chair when he's not in, so shut your fucking face," Ricky said to his brother, then regretted it because he was supposed to be being nice.

"Keep your hair on," Gordon said. "Fucking hell…"

"Pack it in, you two," Mum snapped.

Ricky ignored the pair of them and tucked into his dinner. He reached over to pick up the remote control on the table between the chairs and turned the volume up. All three of them ate in silence, Ricky acutely aware of how *separate* they were, how they'd been that way ever since they'd escaped to Wales, despite Dad's best efforts to knit them into a strong family unit. It could never have happened, Ricky becoming a murderer had seen to that. He wasn't stupid. In reality, he knew they all blamed him for the upheaval in their lives, the feelings they now carried inside them because of him. The memories, the thoughts, the bad dreams.

It was a brilliant feeling to affect so many people like that.

Mum took the remote off the arm of Ricky's chair and turned the telly back down. "I saw you spoke to that Clare woman on Facebook."

"I was going to ignore her but thought it would look weird if I did that."

"Best you don't do it again," Mum said. "You've made her come off as a bit unhinged to be honest, and people will see that. Let that be the only conclusion they come to. The more you speak, the more they'll dig into things. They're already doing it about your father's death. We don't need Clare's son's being brought back up, do we?"

"Fair enough." Ricky bit the end off a large battered sausage.

"Where did you go?" Mum asked.

"Had a few Cokes at the Suits."

She sighed. "I really don't think you should be going there."

"Why not? You said Emma was no one to worry about."

"I know I did, and I stick by that, but with all this shit going round about your dad dying, it's best we keep our heads down."

"Why would we need to do that," Gordon said, "if we've done nothing wrong?"

That was his way of letting Ricky know that he knew they *had* done something wrong. All right, Gordon had only lied by omission by not mentioning the row to the police, and Ricky had been the one to bring about Dad's fall, but for some reason, Gordon had felt the need to have a dig. Maybe he was checking whether Mum suspected Ricky, or maybe he was actually being a good brother and covering up what Ricky had done in front of their mother.

"I'm not stupid, Gordon," she said.

"What are you on about?" he asked.

"I don't want to talk about it." She turned the telly back up.

That could have been her way of saying to Ricky that if he *had* killed his dad, it was okay, he'd done her a massive favour, but not wanting to talk about it meant she didn't want to admit out loud that her son had been capable of ending two lives, both supposed accidents. Maybe she'd been thinking a lot today and had realised that the first one had been an intended kill, too.

"We'll get all this shit over and done with," he said, "the funeral and whatever, and then I'll hire a van to get your stuff moved back to Wales."

Mum glanced at Gordon. "Your brother is coming, too. I've got no problem with it if he's got no problem with me moving on. I refuse to hide my light under a bushel now. If I happen to find a new fella, then that's my lookout. My choice."

Ricky stared across at Gordon. "Are you going because you want to, or have you stepped into Dad's shoes and think she needs protecting?"

"It's shit here. I want to go home."

"How many times did we hear this when we were in Wales? London was home then."

"It's not the same here anymore."

No, it wasn't, but Ricky wouldn't admit he'd made a mistake in wanting to return. It would have been okay if Dad hadn't stuck his oar in and insisted everybody came back en masse. Ricky could have discovered that London wasn't how he'd remembered it and then gone back to Wales. He'd have had his tail tucked between his legs because Dad would have said I told you so, even though *he'd* jumped at the chance to get back to the East End, but the smug taunt would have passed.

He finished eating his dinner and sat sipping his drink, thinking about how he was going to pour acid over the inside of Emma's phone — after he'd watched the footage. It was going to be weird seeing his younger self stabbing that kid.

He still couldn't believe Emma had the balls to video him.

That was one of the things he didn't like in life. You could control people only to a certain point, then they made their own decisions, even if you scared them shitless. Emma had kept the footage despite his dad's warning, and Clare Donaldson had now changed her mind. At the time it happened, she'd been on the news saying she'd accepted it had been a murder committed by a homeless man, so why did she now think it was Ricky? Why was she being so vocal about it? What had she discovered that had given her the idea of who her sons killer really was? Why hadn't the police said anything to him, if she'd even gone to them with her concerns? *Were* they working in the background to find proper proof before they approached him, or were they none the wiser?

He conceded that they would be soon. There had to be a specific officer who monitored social media all day for a living. They'd have already seen her accusation and Ricky's response. He just had to resign himself to the fact that at some point they may pop round to ask him questions. Now he was on their radar because of Dad's death, it might have been inevitable anyway.

He'd memorised what he'd said to the coppers when they'd questioned him about Spencer's murder so he had no problem with repeating it now. He'd been at home with his family and Emma. Hopefully he'd be believed a second time and this would be put back to bed. Clare was going to have to accept that no one else was going to be found guilty. No one else was going to spend time in prison, giving her boy justice.

Not if Ricky could help it.

Emma's phone still had thirty percent battery. In the darkness of his bedroom with earbuds in, Ricky pressed PLAY. The scene appeared on the screen. The back of Ricky as he stood in front of Spencer, the knife in his hand clearly visible.

There were so many things Ricky would change given the chance. He'd have confronted the kid on his own, for a start, keeping Emma out of the loop.

Disappointed that he'd got no satisfaction from watching the video, only a deep sense of annoyance at how he'd played it so wrong, he got up and slipped the phone into his pocket. In the hallway, he put on his shoes and coat and a pair of gloves and, ignoring Mum asking him from the living room where he was going, he left via the front and nipped down the alley between their house and the next, entering the back garden and then the shed where the acid was. Dad had metal containers in there that he stored his screws in. One of them would do to put the phone in and pour the acid on.

Job done, he popped the container at the back of one of the standing shelves Dad had stored his tools on. Ricky would bury the phone when Mum and Gordon were out of the way. For now, he'd leave it hidden and go back to the pub so he could follow Emma home.

He couldn't do that, though. After waiting outside the Suits in the cold, he spotted her getting into a taxi. He trudged back home and, seeing as there were no lights on, he collected the ruined phone from the shed, plus a shovel, and quietly got to work, digging a little grave for it.

Chapter Twenty-One

Emma had the morning off, and she stood in Bespoke Boutique, Amanda's clothing shop. Amanda had put all the new stock out and had finished her extended New Year sale. It would soon be time to think about the spring fashion line, but Emma had to remind herself this wasn't her job anymore.

Amanda sat at her tall white cash desk, filing her nails. It had obviously been a slow morning so far. "So he acted completely normal then."

"He was being nice, but not overly so. Yet at the same time I still don't trust him."

"Of course you don't. No one trusts a murderer."

Amanda hadn't particularly shown much alarm when Emma had confessed her past. She'd been more bothered that Emma hadn't confided in her at the time and that she hadn't even been aware that Emma had been such a cow on the quiet. Amanda had made this about herself and how it affected her, which shouldn't have been a surprise.

"Do you not hate me for my part in it?" Emma asked.

"I could never hate you and I can well imagine how it went. You had no choice but to be there with him. Okay, the police or our mums and dads would say you *did* have a choice, that everyone has one, blah, blah, blah, but when you're in that sort of situation, it's not as easy, is it? Especially when you're a kid. Everything seemed so much more...I don't know, massive then. I mean, I look back at the stuff I used to worry about and it really was stupid shit like whether so-and-so from maths class had given me a filthy look or not. Who gives a shit?"

"I know what you mean, but unfortunately, back then I did have something incredibly awful to worry about."

"How did it feel to only have the McIntyres to speak to about it?"

"I didn't even do that. I avoided them. After… After the body was found. I only spoke to Ricky, and that was when he'd come up to me at school and banged on about me keeping my mouth shut."

"So you coped with it all by yourself."

Emma nodded. It had been so hard. The night it had happened she'd cried. She'd wanted to go downstairs and tell her parents, but seeing the disappointment on their faces had stopped her. She couldn't have done that to them.

"Bloody hell, I'm surprised you're not a basket case," Amanda said. "But you've got me to talk to about it now, so that's something."

"Thanks." Emma glanced out into the street, a shiver going through her because sometimes she forgot Norman was dead and that he wasn't out there watching the shop. "Which brings me to the reason I'm here."

Amanda stopped filing her nails. "What's happened?"

"Have you been keeping an eye on the Facebook page?"

"No. Do I need to?"

"There was another post about Ricky's dad, and Clare Donaldson piped up on it, and he responded. I can see why he did it. If he'd ignored her he'd have looked guilty as fuck, but I'm worried this is going to open a can of worms. You know what people are like, they'll spot that and all dive in."

"When did this happen?"

"Yesterday."

"And what's been said since?"

Emma took her phone out of her pocket and brought up the relevant post. She handed her cousin the mobile then leaned over her shoulder to read the screen.

> *Keith Knowles: Bit below the belt if you don't have proof, Clare.*
>
> *Clare: I'll find it, don't you worry.*

Keith Knowles: I wasn't worried as it happens. I don't think this is the right place to discuss this. If you've got suspicions then you should go to the police.

Clare: I will eventually.

Keith Knowles: I can understand your frustration, but resorting to name-calling isn't going to help either, is it?

Clare: But he IS a little prick.

"That's not so bad," Amanda said. "I was expecting it to be a lot worse. And think about it, why are you fretting about something that's not likely to go anywhere? She says she'll find the proof, which means all she's going on at the moment is the suspicions that Keith bloke mentioned."

"True. It's just that my mind was whirring, probably how yours was with the Norman thing. You think about anything and everything to do with what you're going through. I kept this secret to myself for so many years, so for it to come out now when I've accepted my part in it and forgiven myself, it just seems a bit shit, doesn't it?"

"I've already told you that with no Ricky the problem's solved. He's probably one of those sick types who wanked over that video last night."

"Bloody hell, Amanda, thanks for putting that in my head."

"There's all sorts of shit like that on Netflix. Watch the true crime documentaries, then you'll see." Amanda scrolled and pointed at the screen.

> *Bulldozer Ben: I remember when that happened. Everyone at school was so shocked. But there's no way it would be Ricky. I'm sorry, Clare, but you've got the wrong end of the stick.*
>
>> *Clare: Aren't you brave enough to come on here with your proper name? I bet you're one of the prick's friends, aren't you?*
>
> *Bulldozer Ben: Well, like you're brave enough to put up your surname? And no, I'm not one of his friends. Even if I was, I'd*

be perfectly within my rights to stand up for him.

> *Clare: Like I'm within my rights to say he killed my son.*

Bulldozer Ben: Without proof, I don't think so. What makes you think it was Ricky anyway?

> *Clare: I found a diary. It says my boy was being bullied by him. Ricky tripped him over and stuff like that.*

Bulldozer Ben: Hardly means he's a killer, though, does it?

> *Clare: I WILL prove it, you wait and see.*

"Blimey." Amanda blew out a stream of air. "She's got it in for him, hasn't she? I wonder what that diary said."

"Isn't she a bit thick to be saying that on a public forum, though, considering what Ricky might do about it?"

Amanda's eyes widened. "I'm telling you, if anything happens to Clare because he's gone to her house to get that diary, I *will* be going to the twins."

"Would he risk going there? So many people have video doorbells these days, so would he take the chance of being caught on one of them? If you think about it, he's been worried about the footage I had for years, so to appear on some more… I honestly don't think he's going to pursue this."

"But you're basing that on the Ricky you used to know, not the one he's become."

"What do you want me to do? Talk to him? We don't have each other's phone numbers so I'd have to wait until he came into the pub, and there's no telling he'll even do that now he's got my old mobile. He has what he wanted, so perhaps he'll leave me alone."

"I hope so." Amanda pinched her bottom lip. "This is going to sound mean of me, because you can see how upset Clare is, but I don't want her to find any proof because that means you're going to be dragged into it. There's no way Ricky will keep his mouth shut that you weren't there. Unless, of course, you can convince him in the meantime that you still care about him. If he thinks you love him or whatever, he's more likely to keep you safe."

"One, I won't have time to make him think I love him, and two, I don't particularly want to pretend I do. I don't want him anywhere near me."

"Then you'd better hope Clare's on a mission to nowhere."

Put like that… "Fucking hell, why couldn't the McIntyres have stayed in Wales? Everything was fine until they came back.

Amanda refreshed the screen. "Oh, bloody Nora…"

> *Ricky McIntyre: I'm actually going to go to the police station in a minute and have a chat about this thread. I was already spoken to years ago when your son died, Clare, and it was nothing to do with me. I don't appreciate having my name blackened online, and normally I would shrug it off, but with the recent death of my father, this is adding to my mother's distress. Hopefully the police will be in contact with you soon.*

Clare: You're bluffing.

Ricky McIntyre: Like I said, they'll be in contact with you soon.

"He's very good at pretending, isn't he," Amanda said. "But then again, so are you. I had no idea you were involved in this shit. It's pretty scary when I think about how I didn't have a clue. I thought you were the same old Emma all along."

"I'd have preferred not to have had to pretend, obviously, but I was put in an impossible situation. I wish I'd never met him, but I did, and I kept his secret, and there's nothing I can do about that now."

"I don't want to rub it in or anything, but there's a real possibility now, if he goes to the station, that you'll be questioned. Unless it's like Clare said and he's bluffing."

"Hmm, he could be buying himself time, getting her to shut up for a while so he has a moment to think about how to deal with her."

Amanda gestured to the screen. "Well, he's got enough support, look."

Bulldozer Ben: Good for you, Ricky. No one should be accused of something they haven't done in such a public place.

> *Turd_in_a_Jar: Agreed, Ben. This is how vigilante shit starts, not to mention a person's character torn apart online when everyone else does a massive pile-on. Clare, if you've got concerns then go to the police, but it looks like they're going to be paying you a visit anyway.*

Glorious Cakes: Sorry, but coming on here to accuse someone isn't the way to do it, Clare. Have a heart. The poor bloke's dad's only just died.

> *Clare: Poor bloke? He's a KILLER!!!*

Bulldozer Ben: So you say.

"Clare might go quiet when she sees the support isn't for her but for him," Amanda said. "I can't believe I just said that because it sounds like I'm on Ricky's side, but I'm not, I'm only concerned about you and making sure you're safe from being dragged into it. I still say we ought to get Ricky dealt with, but I understand why you don't want that, I really do. But let me just say this: we could word it in such a way that the twins feel sorry for you and think you've been wronged, like Ricky forced you to be there when he killed Spencer. I know you said you went there for kicks, but you didn't expect him to actually go through with it, did you? And that's a big difference. Yes, they're going to want to know why you kept your mouth shut all these years, but isn't it obvious? And anyway, with Mr McIntyre dead, you can make up any old bullshit about something he supposedly said to you years ago, even though he didn't. It's not like he's here to refute it, is it? Think about it, okay? Because if Clare pursues this, or she even goes to the police herself to call Ricky's bluff, then everything could get out of hand pretty bloody quickly."

"Okay, I'll think about it."

"Promise?"

"Honestly, I will. The walls are starting to close in."

"I know Mrs McIntyre and Gordon are what's stopping you, but they were involved, too, don't forget."

"Bullied by Verne, though. They probably didn't have a choice either. I was there, remember? I saw how they were afraid of him, and I knew all about how he behaved at home because Ricky told me he hated him, and I've got an awful feeling he actually pushed his dad off that railing last night."

"Fucking hell, then he's dangerous and you really do need to get this sorted."

Emma nodded. "I have to go to work now. I'll mull it over and let you know."

"Come to mine again after your shift. We'll get a takeaway and talk it through. I know we've already done that, but we need to make a proper plan. Things have escalated since then."

Emma put her phone in her pocket and gave Amanda a hug. She left the shop, glad to be out in the cold fresh air to clear her head. Now this crap had seeped online again after all these years, and despite Ricky trying to put out the flames, Emma had a horrible feeling it would only escalate, given time. For a few seconds, she had the urge to change direction and walk to the police station, asking to see DS Colin Broadly, but she forced herself towards the Suits, her head down, the knot of anxiety in her stomach growing tighter.

Muscle memory took her to the pub, and as she looked up to cross the road, she came to a quick stop. Ricky stood in front of her, his face a picture of concern.

"Have you seen online?" he asked. "It's getting worse."

She nodded, took his arm, and steered him over to the pub. She led him around the back so they could talk in private, but first she looked through a knothole in the gate to make sure no one was outside having a break and could overhear them.

"People are sticking up for you, though," she whispered. "And are you really going to go to the police?"

"I spoke to them about it as soon as I mentioned doing it. They were at our house anyway, speaking to Mum."

She didn't want to ask what that was about. The horrible, sneaky feeling that he'd killed his own father wouldn't go away, and she didn't want to be involved with that after the fact. "What did they say?"

"They'll have a quick look at the file, bring my name up, see what went on, then go around and ask her to *refrain*, was how they put it, from making accusations."

"Did they look as though they thought what she'd said had any merit?"

"No, they rolled their eyes as if she was one of those online crackpots. I think we're safe."

"We'll be okay," she said. "We weren't suspected then, so there's no reason why we should be suspected now just because a grieving mother has piped up. Silly cow."

Oh God, she hated herself for sounding like the old Emma, but it had been worth it because Ricky smiled. She'd roped him into believing she was on his side.

"Did you see what she said about the diary and the bullying?" he asked. "My guts went over at that."

So he's scared? He has proper feelings? "But if Spencer had written anything incriminating in there, she'd have taken it to the police, wouldn't she? And she hasn't. She said she'd *find* the proof, which means she hasn't got any at the moment.

Honest to God, the daft bitch is grasping at straws. She must still be devastated, she'll never get over it, but the police went with the homeless man as the killer, and she ought to just accept that."

"You could go online and say that for me."

"Me?"

"Yeah, make a new account."

"That's not going to work."

"Why not?"

"Because a lot of people follow profiles after reading incendiary comments. Once someone says something, they'll see I don't have any posts and the account is new. Even if I do stick a couple of posts up, it's going to be obvious it's a puppet account. That's how I knew the anon messages you sent me were from someone trying to hide themselves. Clare could start a rumour that the new account is you when it actually isn't, and that's not going to look very good, is it, because the police already know you made an account to harass *me*."

Ricky's grin lit up his face. "And this is why we were so good together back then. You point shit out that I don't even think about."

"So we're agreed that I'm not going to leave a comment then, yes?"

"Yeah."

"Just let the police deal with her. If all they manage to do is get her to shut up online, then we can call it job done." She glanced at the gate. "I'd better go. I have to start work."

"Thanks for making me see sense," he said and walked off.

Emma went around the corner and entered the pub from the front. Liz gave her a wave, and Kenny nodded his greeting. Emma went behind the bar and into the staffroom to hang her coat up and pop her bag in her locker. She still had twenty minutes left before her shift started, so she made a coffee and sat at the table.

It *would* be okay, wouldn't it?

She shivered at the not knowing.

Chapter Twenty-Two

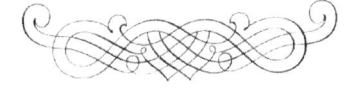

Clare sat at her dining room table and read the diary again. She knew the words off by heart but, desperate to spot something she may have missed the other countless times she'd studied them, she read them again. Nothing. They were exactly the same as before. Sometimes she wished her son would give her a sign, although maybe he had because she thought she'd gone through his bedroom with a fine-tooth comb, not to mention the police doing the same, and yet that diary had remained hidden. She'd only found it when her toe had stubbed on something as she'd stood at his bedroom window. She'd looked down to see nothing on the rug and realised it was something *underneath* it.

She'd got on her knees and slid the slim item out, and at first she'd just stared at it where it lay on the floor, knowing it may contain the precious proof she needed. But at the same time, she didn't know whether she wanted to be made aware.

For years, she had tirelessly kept her son's case relevant and in the forefront of people's minds, doing newspaper articles every so often, and her blog had migrated to a Facebook page dedicated to her boy. So she'd picked up the exercise book and began to read, and the one thing that had stood out throughout that whole year was Ricky McIntyre had bullied Spencer relentlessly. Every single school day and at the weekend if he happened to bump into him.

It had made sense why Spencer had taken to keeping himself indoors, sparing himself from any attacks he may receive on a weekday evening and Saturday and Sunday if there weren't teachers or people on hand to stand up for him. She'd assumed he'd just gone insular; some teenagers tended to do that. Her elder daughter, Heidi, had done the same, so why would Clare have thought her son would be any different? Heidi's teenage years were all Clare had to go on when Spencer had entered them, too. It was as if she'd followed the guidebook belonging to Heidi's teens when really she should have asked herself whether boys and girls were different, whether Spencer staying indoors was a cause for concern.

But she hadn't.

There were so many things she hadn't done and so many things she had. Regrets strangled her every day for some of them, her throat so tight with emotion she couldn't breathe. If only she hadn't been so pleased that he'd wanted to go out that night. If only she hadn't chivvied him out of the door. But he was happy, unless it was faked for her benefit, to be going to his friend's birthday party at the bowling alley. Clare had been relieved that her son had wanted to leave his room and get dressed in nice clothes. She'd thought he was turning a corner, but the last diary entry proved otherwise.

> *I'm really worried about bumping into Ricky tonight. Jordan said he hasn't invited him to the party, but he lies sometimes. He might have said it to get me to come. Not that Jordan would get Ricky there on purpose so he could beat me up, it's just I don't trust anyone anymore apart from Mum and Dad and Heidi. So why haven't I told them about the bullying? I don't want Mum to worry, and Dad would go round to Ricky's and start a fight. Mr McIntyre is an arsehole, and Dad could get hurt. Fucking hell, why did I say I'd go? I should have had the guts to say I wanted to stay at home.*

Clare wiped the tears from her eyes. "You said you'd go because you listened to me when I told you it'd be fun. I wish I'd never said it, son. Jesus Christ, why didn't I keep my mouth shut?"

But there was cause to open it now. Surely, if she spoke to the right police officer, one who actually wanted to listen instead of brushing her off, they'd speak to Ricky about what Spencer had written. There was no way Ricky had meant it on Facebook when he'd said he'd tell the police about her accusation. He wouldn't want to expose what he'd done, especially because she'd mentioned a diary at some point, although to be fair, he might not have seen that bit. If he had, though? He must be a right cocky bastard not to be worrying about what could be revealed about him.

She got up and put the diary in the sideboard. Although the bullying had been documented, some people would say it was 'just the usual kind of thing between kids', it wasn't anything major: tripping Spencer over, poking him in the back, saying mean things. While it had clearly affected Spencer to the point he'd made himself a recluse after school and at weekends, there had been no mention of death threats or fights or anything of a violent nature, so in a way, she could understand why the officers she'd spoken to already had put the bullying down to two teenage lads just not getting on.

But this was how more dramatic bullying started. Bullies always escalated, and even though Ricky had an alibi, she didn't believe it.

He'd said he hadn't even gone out that night, he'd been at home with his family and that Emma girl, the little bitch. She was with Ricky a couple of times when he'd bullied Spencer. Clare had told the police about her, too, but the officer had pointed out that if Emma was just in the vicinity and hadn't said or done anything, while it was obvious she was friends with a bully, it didn't mean she was a bully herself.

Clearly, those two officers had never experienced anything like it themselves.

Clare made up her mind. She took the diary back out and put it in her handbag. She was going to walk to the police station and ask to speak to somebody who actually had proper knowledge of bullying and how it could get worse and end fatally. Someone in that station must be trained in that sort of thing.

In the hallway, she popped her shoes on, and just as she reached out to take her coat off the hook on the wall, two black shapes on the other side of the glass in the front door caught her attention. A shadowy arm raised to ring the bell, but she opened the door before the finger could make contact. Two police officers in uniform stood there, and she knew then that Ricky had stuck to his word.

"Mrs Clare Donaldson?" the young blond fella said.

She nodded. "Are you here about that fucking Ricky McIntyre? Are you going to fuck me off, tell me to shut up? Well, let me tell you, I'll *never* shut up, not when it comes to my son. He was murdered, that's not in dispute, but it wasn't some homeless man, it was Ricky."

"Mr McIntyre has made us aware of what you've said online. We've come here to take a statement."

"A statement?"

"As to why you think he killed your son."

Oh, well, she hadn't expected that. "Can I see some ID?"

The pair of them showed it to her and, satisfied they were the real deal, she let them into her kitchen and took the diary out of her bag. She placed it on the table and jabbed a finger on the front.

"That's proof enough for me, but not for a couple of coppers I saw last week after I found that diary. Do you want a cup of tea?"

"That would be lovely, thank you."

"Are you really here to help me? Or to try to get me to shut up?"

"It's a serious allegation you've made, Mrs Donaldson, so we've been instructed to get to the bottom of it."

She smiled. "Then you can call me Clare."

Chapter Twenty-Three

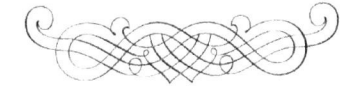

The night of Jordan's birthday party had arrived. Emma hadn't been invited, so she'd told her parents she was going to Laura's. Ricky and Jordan didn't move in the same circles, so there was no way Ricky had got an invite either. He'd said they should meet in the tree clearing, drink some booze he'd nicked

(only enough to get tipsy), then they could gate-crash the party for a laugh.

Emma didn't want to do that. It was the night she'd decided to tell him she wasn't allowed to hang around with him anymore, that someone had grassed them up, seen them together, and Dad had told her to go and tell Ricky they had to part ways. All the way to the clearing, she rehearsed how she was going to broach the subject.

Oh my God, you'll never guess what happened. Someone told my dad I haven't been with Laura, I was with a boy, and he's gone mad...

I can't see you anymore. My dad's found out about us. Sorry.

Someone rang my house anonymously and told my mum and dad I've been with you. There's no way I can hang around with you anymore.

Whatever way she said it, it sounded like a lie to her. But maybe that was because she knew it was. If she was hearing someone else say something like that to her, of course she'd believe them, but this was Ricky they were talking about, Mr Suspicious, someone who thought everything through, picking it apart until he found the lie. But she couldn't tell him she didn't want to hang out with him anymore and it was her decision. He'd get shitty with her and maybe bully her like he did with

Spencer. But did that matter? There was only a few months left at school now. She could put up with him being cruel and saying nasty shit until the exams were over and then she'd never have to see him again.

Her stomach clenched uncomfortably when the trees came into view. She walked across the grass towards them, glancing back over her shoulder at two girls and a lad of about seventeen who sat on the swings talking. At least if Ricky turned funny, Emma could run out and get help, but what if he was too quick for her and he stopped her leaving the clearing? He could put hand over her mouth, no trouble, and stop her from making a noise. He could strangle her like he wanted to strangle their geography teacher. He could bring a knife and stab her like he wanted to stab Spencer. He could have a jumbo sausage and—

Stop being so fucking stupid.

She marched into the clearing, full of forced confidence, only to find he wasn't there. Now it could be her turn to make a sarky comment about him being late, but honestly, she couldn't be bothered. The quicker she told him this was over, the quicker she could get home and return to the boring life she'd led before she'd got involved with him.

She wasn't going to sit on the damp grass in the absence of his piece of tarpaulin, and didn't that make him a weirdo anyway? What sort of kid carried that around with them?

She shuddered at the answer he would likely have given her to that question: "It's just in case I kill someone, isn't it? I could wrap them up in it after." It wasn't big enough for that, unless it was an animal or a small child, but whatever, it still gave her the creeps.

She stepped out of the clearing, unwilling to wait in there by herself in case he was being a prick and hiding behind one of the tree trunks, watching her. She'd caught him doing that a few times. Not hiding behind tree trunks but the watching, as if he sized her up. Or maybe he had thoughts of murdering her *and he'd only made friends with her so he could butter her up. Get her to trust him and then he'd strike.*

And no matter how much she'd like to say that was a stupid notion, after the hundreds of conversations she'd had with him, she knew it wasn't. He was very much the type to befriend someone, then he flipped a switch and became a completely different person.

The girls and the boy were still on the swings, their low laughter and conversation floating over, but she couldn't make out what they were saying. A marching silhouette caught her attention to the right, the same shape as Ricky, the streetlight at the alley entrance that joined the park to the housing estate illuminating him from behind. Emma's heart hammered, and the strong urge to run took over her, to the point she moved one foot forward but then stopped herself. She had to do this. She wouldn't abandon him like he'd left her in that building. She'd at least have the decency to explain she wouldn't be meeting him anymore. The reason for it would be a lie, but that didn't matter.

She'd do it outside the clearing, so when he entered the tree line and she didn't follow, he stopped to look back at her.

"What's the matter?" he asked.

"I've got to tell you something."

"Can I go first?" He walked back out to join her.

It wouldn't hurt, would it, for him to say what he had to say. She could at least gauge what mood he was in then.

"Go on then," she said.

"Spencer is definitely going to Jordan's party."

"So?"

"Like I said, we're going crash it, and Spencer being there is all the more reason to do it."

"I don't want to be horrible to him," she said.

"Oh, come on, it'll be a right laugh. I've even bought balaclavas so nobody knows who we are."

She shook her head. "But that's stupid. Why bother putting a balaclava on if we're just turning up at a party uninvited? What's the bloody problem with people knowing who we are?"

Ricky took a deep breath. "Because I'm going to kill him tonight."

Emma's guts went south. "No. I'm absolutely not having anything to do with this." She backed away from him.

Ricky caught up with her, reached out to grasp her wrist, squeezing it tight over the sleeve of her jacket. Despite the puffy lining, it still hurt.

Emma flinched. "You're doing to me what you said your dad does to your mum."

He snatched his hand off her. "Look, I was joking, okay? I'm not going to kill him. I mean, there'll be too many people there for a start."

"Which is why you mentioned the balaclavas. I'm going home. If you choose to go to the party, that's your problem."

She headed towards the people on the swings, then she stopped and turned to him. He was right there *where he must have followed her. She hid her shock.*

"Oh, I forgot to tell you my thing. Someone told my parents I haven't been seeing Laura. They're so angry I lied and I've been doing it for ages. I got in the shit because they wanted to know where I was that night when you left me in the building."

"Did you say you were with me?" He gripped her wrist again. *"I swear to God, Emma, if you did and my dad finds out what we've been up to, I'm dead."*

"Your dad won't kill you."

"No, but I'll be in serious trouble."

"Don't you dare say what 'we've' been up to. It's you who's been doing stuff. I've just watched."

"It doesn't matter. You were with me and didn't stop it, so that means you're still involved. So what happens now? Are you going to go home and we don't speak to each other again after all the shit we've talked about? How can I trust you not to tell anybody?"

"The same way you could trust me before. Just because I'm not allowed to see you, it doesn't mean I'm going to tell everyone what you dream about doing to people."

"Stay out with me, just this one last night. What's your dad going to do? Ground you for an extra week? At least then we'd have had a bloody good laugh and it'll give us something to think about later on."

Seeing as she'd just lied her face off, it wasn't going to make any difference whether she stayed out or not, but to maintain the charade, she said, "Okay, but he expects me to tell him who you are when I get home. I'm not going to, obviously, because he might go round to speak to your mum, and then it'll cause trouble if your dad finds out."

"Okay."

"So what do you want to do then, still gate-crash the party?"

"Nah, we'll hang around outside it. Follow Spencer home."

"Swear to me you won't kill him."

Ricky let out a pop of laughter. "Come on. One last night of fun."

Chapter Twenty-Four

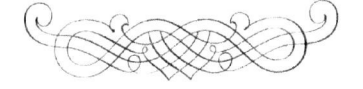

Why couldn't people just leave shit the fuck alone? The coppers Ricky had spoken to had got back to him. Their senior officer had decided that as Clare had made an allegation of murder, then instead of a quick warning to tell her to pack it in, they were looking into it more closely. Ricky's confidence in the situation had depleted rapidly, and now he had to worry about what Clare had told the police. She'd given a statement, apparently, about the diary—so *was* there something in it of use with regards to pinning the murder on him? No, a dead teenager couldn't write in his diary, saying Ricky had killed him. Spencer had no idea he was going to be killed prior to the event itself, so this latest turn of events didn't make sense.

Unless Spencer had been a clever little cunt and documented the bullying. Back then it would have been classed as boys being boys, but these days bullying was looked at more seriously. Everything was looked at more seriously because of the whiny, entitled brats who screeched about the value of their mental health every chance they got. You got "me" days. You got days off work just because you didn't feel like going and it might make you cry if you did. Everyone was such a fucking snowflake. It did his head in.

So the words of a dead kid were what would bring Ricky down, were they? Maybe he should sit and cry like everyone else did, drown in self-pity, throw himself down on the sofa and demand smelling salts. Fuck's sake. No, sod that. What was it Dad had always said? "If you eliminate the problem, then there's no longer a problem." But Mum had piped up with, "True, but then you create another problem if you've got to hide the fact you've got rid of the first one."

And getting rid of Clare seemed to be the only option at the minute. He'd done a bit of snooping on the page she'd created for Spencer. She documented everything and used it as a public diary where she expressed her thoughts and feelings regularly, so it hadn't been hard to discover that her obsession with finding Spencer's killer had led to her husband walking out on her and her daughter barely coming to see her. Clare had suffered a mental breakdown, which was handy and went in Ricky's favour—what she said might be scrutinised more carefully now. But there was the diary. Her sanity wouldn't affect what it said, it was a piece of evidence in its own right, so whether or not she'd gone doolally at some point didn't matter.

He'd bet the police had it now. They'd likely pay him a visit tomorrow and question him about the bullying. He was going to have to make out he'd just been an arsehole teenager who'd picked on Spencer for fun, there was nothing more to it than that. He couldn't admit it was because he was jealous of the kid who'd always got what he wanted for Christmas and he walked around in name-brand clothes and trainers instead of the cheap copies everyone else had. He didn't go without, and his parents really gave a shit about him. Spencer hadn't bragged or anything, his home life had become evident at registration every Monday when the teacher asked how their weekend had gone. He'd always piped up with some bollocks or other. Amazing how he never came off as braggy, just stating facts.

The old coil of anger unfurled inside Ricky. Remembering those days wasn't advisable because it usually sent him off on one. And it was annoying because he'd just got his head sorted after talking to Emma and getting rid of her mobile, and now this Clare shit.

He had a look online to check the state of play. She hadn't added any more titbits to the comment section of either post about his dad, but she *had* put up an entry on Spencer's page.

> *It's been an emotional day. Or should I say another one. Do you remember I said about that boy who'd murdered Spencer? I've never named him here, but I lost control on*

a local page and blurted that I thought he'd killed my son. He responded at some point, had the bloody cheek to say he was sorry for my loss or something like that—talk about make my skin crawl. Anyway, I've ended up speaking to the police. The decision was taken out of my hands because he contacted them first. Owing to my allegation, the police have chosen to look into it more carefully and are now in possession of the diary. I'm hoping Spencer's words are proof enough that my son was unhappy in the last few months of his life and that he did not want to go to that final birthday party because of a certain person. That is all I'm prepared to say on the matter at the moment as the investigation is ongoing. I'm praying it has the outcome I so sorely need.

She'd given just enough information to let Ricky know exactly how things were going. There was no proof he'd killed her son, just a dead boy's ramblings about being picked on. When the police came to see him, which they would if they thought her allegation had wings, at some point he'd slip it in there about the homeless man who'd been convicted of the murder. The whole original investigation had pointed to it being the tramp—an eyewitness in the graveyard had seen him going down the alley, then coming back out half an hour later. They clearly hadn't seen Ricky and Emma, they must have been too busy with their girlfriend behind that angel monument, but Ricky wasn't going to complain about it.

Deep in his gut, he felt this would all blow over. Back then, they hadn't been able to prove he wasn't at home that night, and he doubted very much they could prove it now. Were they really going to reopen the investigation and poke into it when it had a satisfying conclusion the first time round? He remembered some bloke high up in the police going on the telly and saying the case had come to an end.

Maybe it would be better if he got rid of Clare, but first he'd have to dig the mobile back up and get rid of it elsewhere. The fingers of blame were definitely going to point in his direction if she turned up dead, and who knew whether the police would want to search the house and garden.

He checked his watch. He just had enough time to catch B&Q before it closed at eight. He'd buy a rose bush and plant it where he'd dug the hole for the phone, then there'd be no questions from the police as to why the earth had been disturbed. This way he could say he'd bought the bush in memory of his father.

And no one could prove otherwise.

Chapter Twenty-Five

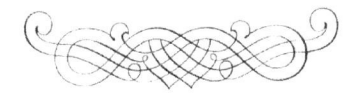

Emma and Amanda had scoured Facebook for any new snippets from Clare, and they discovered a page dedicated to Spencer Donaldson. It mentioned the diary and the descriptions of bullying contained within it. Emma's name had also been mentioned, but not her surname. That was something, at least. But as

Ricky had told her that he'd informed the police about Clare's allegation, plus Clare herself had written about it, what if they wanted to know who Emma was? What if they contacted him and asked, then he told them? Or they could easily find out by looking at the old file and seeing her name in it and that her alibi was that she'd been round Ricky's house all evening.

"You're going to have to give in and ring the twins," Amanda said. "You can't afford to leave this now. Ricky could lead the police right to your door to get the spotlight off himself. George and Greg need to get rid of him before he can do that."

"But if he blames me for it then he risks me opening my mouth and telling the police it was him. We're both kind of stuck backing each other up, even if we don't want to. But yes, I agree, this is all going too far. God, why can't the past just stay there?"

"I thought exactly the same thing—you know, because of Norman. If he'd left the past alone then he'd never have come into my house without me knowing about it, and that crap that followed wouldn't have happened." Amanda paused. "Do you want me to get hold of them for you?"

"No, I need to sort this out myself." Emma already had their phone number in her contacts list because they'd given it to her when she'd been interviewed for her job at the Suits. "I just don't know how I'm going to put it."

"Maybe tell them you need to speak to them urgently but don't say why—do it in a message. Say you're best telling them face to face, they'll know it's serious then."

Emma nodded and typed it out. Pressing SEND turned her stomach over, but it was done now, no taking it back. The message tone seemed to blare out far too loudly, and she stared at Amanda, her heart rate escalating.

Amanda flapped a hand. "Open the bloody thing to see what they've said then!"

Fingers shaking, Emma did what she'd been told.

GG: How important is it? We've got a fish dangling on a hook, and before you ask, that's a metaphor.

Emma: You asked me if I had a secret and I said no. I lied.

GG: And the secret is about to bite you on the arse, I take it.

Emma: Yes, and it'll be a big chunk.

GG: I'M SURPRISED YOU CAN'T HEAR MY SIGH FROM WHERE YOU ARE. WHICH IS?

EMMA: AMANDA'S.

GG: DO WE HAVE ENOUGH TIME FOR ME TO DISPOSE OF THE FISH?

EMMA: YES. I DON'T THINK ANYTHING WILL HAPPEN THAT QUICKLY, AS IN THE POLICE COMING TO TALK TO ME TONIGHT. AS I'M NOT AT HOME, THEY WOULDN'T BE ABLE TO GET HOLD OF ME UNTIL TOMORROW ANYWAY, BUT I COULD HOLE UP AT AMANDA'S UNTIL IT'S SAFE TO COME BACK OUT AGAIN.

GG: GREG HERE. GEORGE IS NOW DEALING WITH THE FISH. WE'LL BE OVER AS SOON AS WE CAN. SIT TIGHT, BUT FAIR WARNING, HE'S MORE PISSED OFF THAN I AM THAT YOU LIED TO US. JUST THINK, IF YOU'D HAVE REVEALED YOUR SECRET WHEN WE SPOKE TO YOU IN THE JOB INTERVIEW, I DOUBT VERY MUCH WE'D BE HAVING THIS CONVERSATION NOW BECAUSE WE'D HAVE DEALT WITH THE ISSUE BACK THEN. STILL, WE LIVE AND LEARN, DON'T WE.

Emma looked at her cousin, tears filling her eyes.

"Well?" Amanda said. "What did they have to say?"

Emma passed her phone over and left the room to go and make a cup of tea. She'd always wondered whether karma would catch up with her, if it would wait then crawl out to capture her when she least expected it. She'd said sorry in her head a million times over for how she'd behaved when hanging around with Ricky and had stupidly thought that would be enough.

Wasn't guilt and remorse a tough enough lesson?

And now she was going to have some more to add to her already large pile. She was going to ask the twins to kill Ricky, maybe go round and see Clare to shut her the fuck up, too.

What a sodding mess.

Chapter Twenty-Six

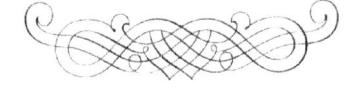

The body lay at the bottom of the stairs in its final resting place from where he'd pushed her at the top. The stupid bitch had no security at her house and had even left the back door open so he could just walk right in. If she was so worried about him being a murderer, someone who'd take offence at the things she'd been saying online, he'd have thought she would worry he'd come after her. Maybe she'd forgotten to lock up, but whatever, her lapse in security was his gain.

The scene at home was perfect when he'd left. Mum and Gordon had gone to bed early, and he'd made out he was doing the same. He'd waited until the pair of them were snoring and then got out of bed around ten, dressed all in black, and walked to Clare's with his head down. He had no idea whether she still lived there but had taken a punt—he'd imagined she wouldn't want to leave the place where her son had grown up.

Music still blared from upstairs. Earlier, he'd gone up there guessing she'd kept Spencer's bedroom as a shrine. Ricky had found her sitting on the bed and sobbing loudly, hands over her face. He'd gathered the music was to hide the crying from the neighbours—a bit like when women cried in the shower so the water disguised their tears. It was so noisy that it had been easy to walk in without her hearing or seeing him. She had her back to the door, and he'd snatched her hair in his fist. She'd lowered her hands immediately and took a deep breath to scream, but he'd slapped a gloved palm over it, hoping it didn't leave any marks for a pathologist to find. He needed this death to look as natural as possible. Another accident. The hair…he worried about some of it breaking from the root, but if he gripped the other side it would look like she'd snatched at her hair herself with both hands in a moment of madness.

He'd placed a few strands between her fingers. Left the music on and walked downstairs, stepping over her body and leaving the same way as he'd come in. In the alley behind the back garden, he looked left and right to check for anyone coming home from either work or the pub. It was clear, so he darted along it and out into a side street, and again, head down, he took an all-over-the-place route so he didn't form a direct path from Clare's to home.

He made it back an hour after he'd left.

His family still snored.

Chapter Twenty-Seven

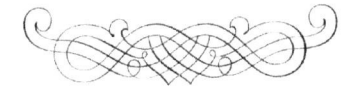

The 'fish' dangling from the hook dangled no more. Unfortunately, George's plan to go slow while torturing him had been changed due to Emma's messages. What the fucking hell had she got herself into? He had to appease himself that there may be another fish to hook up soon, but that would depend on what that fish had done. Maybe she just needed someone warned—that Ricky McIntyre? It was weird how she hadn't said anything about him while they'd been doing shit for her cousin, but then again, maybe she'd kept it to herself so they could concentrate on finding Norman Wagstaff and putting an end to his murdering ways.

With the trapdoor washed and now locked, and a message sent to the crew to come down and bleach the cellar level of the warehouse, George removed his bloodied forensic suit, bagged it up, and had a shower. They had a wood-burning stove being fitted tomorrow, so there would be no more taking evidence home to burn it. George was all about making life easier.

Satisfied everything was in order, he nodded at Greg for them to leave the warehouse. He sat in the passenger seat of their little van and took out two wigs and beards, passing one set to Greg when he got in. They didn't need any of Amanda's neighbours clocking The Brothers turning up.

Suitably disguised, they stared at each other and said what needed to be said without words. They'd see what Emma had to say before giving her a bollocking—whatever had happened to her might mean said bollocking should be put on the back burner or not be spoken at all. Greg nodded and started the engine, driving away while George thought about the scrote whose body parts currently danced in the choppy Thames.

This one was nothing to do with protection money. He'd been a bit violent with one of the women from Kitchen Street. How thick could you get, doing that when you'd handed over your name and registration number, as per the rules if you wanted to use one of the sex workers there? The bloke had said he'd never hurt a woman before, but she'd said something that had set him off, and he'd been as shocked and surprised as she was when he'd lashed out and punched her. He had no idea her words would have triggered him, had no idea he even had something to be triggered about, but apparently, having his mum walk out on him, never to be seen again, hurt more than he'd thought. The sex worker had said if he didn't make up his mind on what he wanted from her, she was getting out of the car. Innocent words that had resulted in his death.

While George could understand the knee-jerk reaction, it was by no means acceptable. He hadn't meant to kill him, just fuck him over a bit while he'd been hanging from the chains, but Emma's messages... He'd needed to get rid of the man as quickly as possible.

One by one, George was determined to remove all the deviants from the Cardigan Estate until they had a relatively nice bunch of residents. But when people like Emma and Amanda popped up in the middle of their mission to clean up the East End, it was more slow going than he'd like.

"What do you reckon her secret is then?" Greg asked. "She forgot to scan an item in Tesco and is now riddled with guilt? She told a lie when she was five and it's bothered her ever since?"

"Pack it in with taking the piss," George said. "It could be serious if she's got hold of us two."

"True, but I was trying to lighten the mood before we once again dive into drama."

George glanced at the dashboard clock. "I doubt very much Colin's at work at this time of night, unless he's got a new murder to deal with, so here's hoping he's not needed until tomorrow, eh?"

They continued on in silence. George appreciated the few moments of peace and quiet, and then they were pulling up outside Amanda's house, somewhere he'd hoped they'd never be again. But life was a funny little bitch with her tricks, twists, and turns, and here they were, about to step into fuck knows what.

"Remember," Greg warned, "be patient and listen first."

George snorted and got out of the van.

Chapter Twenty-Eight

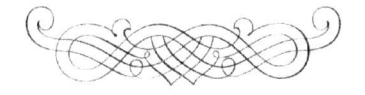

It was altogether too weird to be standing there with a balaclava on. Emma had protested about putting hers over her face instead of just wearing it like a beanie hat, but Ricky had got his own way, as usual. Besides, they were standing in a cobbled alley between two office buildings, in darkness opposite the bowling alley that was a vibrant splash of colour with red and

purples in the neon sign. They'd already seen the birthday party going on, and Emma had felt particularly sorry for Spencer, who'd turned up on his own in a taxi. Was the poor kid so worried about Ricky that he didn't want to be alone, even in public? How come he hadn't arrived with one of his mates? Or did he feel that was still a risk, that two or three lads against Ricky was no match?

How horrible that Emma had been hanging around with a thug and thinking it was cool. But that wasn't the complete truth. She'd always had reservations, she'd just chosen to ignore them. But look how he'd persuaded her to do what he wanted again, and he hadn't even had to try very hard. But once more she'd told herself it would be easier to indulge him. Stupid of her, really, when he'd mentioned killing Spencer again.

What if he did something to him when they followed him home, something other than saying mean things? What if it turned nasty? Then she reminded herself he'd come here in a taxi, so maybe he'd booked one to take him home, too. Ricky wouldn't be able to do what he wanted then.

Unless he already knew Spencer would be walking.

That brought on an unexpected chill, and she shivered. "How do you know he's going to be walking home?"

"Someone happened to mention it."

"Who?"

"It doesn't matter."

"Did you ask them or did you overhear them?"

"Playing devil's advocate again?"

"Someone has to."

"Sounds to me like you're interested in what I might be doing."

"What do you mean, might? You said you weren't. I'm going home if you're going to cross the line. Honestly, we're fifteen. We could be forty by the time we get out of prison. Do you honestly want to spend that amount of time in there?"

"We wouldn't get caught, though. The balaclavas, the gloves."

She puffed out a scornful laugh. "You can't tell me he's going to walk home on his own. Not when you've been bullying him for so long. He got a cab here, for fuck's sake, that's how scared he is."

"If it's meant to be then it'll work out."

That was the kind of saying he must have heard from an adult, and it sounded weird coming out of Ricky's mouth. She stared across at the bowling alley.

The front was mainly windows, a large one each side of the door. Towards the front of the interior, people sat and ate at dining tables, and at the back, people threw bowling balls down the lanes. Emma had been here before with Amanda ages ago. They'd had chicken wings and hot dogs with a bag of candyfloss to share for pudding.

It was going to be yonks before the party was over. She leaned a shoulder on the wall and settled into the darkness of the alley, preparing herself for a long wait. But why should she? Why was she even here?

Because she believed Ricky did have it in mind to kill Spencer and she wanted to be able to stop him. To talk him out of it.

"I still don't believe your excuse for wanting to kill him," she said. "You want to murder someone because they've got a face you want to punch? Is that the excuse you'd give to the police when you got arrested?"

"I wouldn't get arrested."

"You don't know that."

"I wouldn't kill him out in the open where just anyone could walk by and see it."

"Where would you do it then?"

"Isn't it obvious?"

"In the tree clearing?"

"Oh, fuck me. Shut up now, he's coming out, look."

Emma peered over at the bowling alley. Spencer left the venue, shoving his arms into his coat sleeves and rushing to the left. Why was he in such a hurry? Had something happened to upset him? Another alley was down where he'd gone, and a bus stop, so maybe he'd had enough and wanted to go home. Ricky stepped out of their alley, his head up because he didn't have to shield his face with that balaclava on, and walked along the dark pavement. This was Emma's chance to distance herself from what he was about to do. If he really had the balls to do it. Oh God, one minute she thought he did and the next she didn't.

Fuck it.

She went after him, going quickly and hoping she was enough of a black blob in the balaclava and her clothing that her shape wouldn't be recognised, and that wasn't a paranoid thought, because she recognised Ricky's all the time. She darted left into the alley, spotting Ricky at the end of it but no Spencer. She ran to catch up, her footsteps loud and clattering in the confined space where two buildings either side rose four stories high. She came abreast of Ricky, and with her head down but her eyes up, she spotted Spencer across the street. He walked fast. Or maybe that was a slow jog. And she sensed he knew they were there. Not who they were, obviously, because of the disguises, but that someone was in the vicinity. He glanced across at them, his eyes widening, probably at the balaclavas, and then he broke into a proper run.

Ricky shot after him, Emma close behind. Her chest hurt from the spurt of exercise, and she thought about stopping, of going home, but she couldn't leave Spencer with Ricky.

They trailed him through the maze-like backstreets that butted against the rear gardens of homes, and there were so many alleys she lost count and didn't know where she was, her bearings completely shot. They spewed out of yet another alley, and then she knew exactly where she was. Opposite the building where she'd spent the night alone. None of the homeless were around, thank God. Spencer was just turning into the alley. Ricky and Emma went after him. At the halfway mark, Ricky pounced. He landed on Spencer's back, and Emma opened the gate. Spencer struck out blindly, Ricky's hands over his eyes, and she grabbed at his wrist to pull the pair of them through the opening, then slammed the gate shut. Ricky got off him and pushed Spencer towards the door with the padlock.

"Please, just let me go home," Spencer said.

Emma wasn't about to answer. She didn't want to give away her voice, and Ricky kept his mouth shut, too. He prodded Spencer in the back until they reached the door, then he ushered him inside. Emma closed the door. Ricky stood behind Spencer, yanked his balaclava off and put it in his pocket, then chivvied him forward into the room on the right, the one with the tattered pieces of paper on the floor. He kicked the back of Spencer's knee, and Spencer went down.

"Stay there, facedown, and don't move," Ricky said. He took his torch out of his pocket and shone the light on Spencer.

"I want my mum," Spencer wailed.

Emma felt really sorry for him. "That's enough now," she whispered to Ricky. "It's not funny anymore."

"Who's laughing?" Ricky held something up in his other hand, wafting it in and out of the torchlight.

Fucking hell, he had a knife.

"Don't," she said quietly, hoping Ricky heard her over Spencer's sobs.

"This is our last night together," Ricky said. "We have to make it special."

"I won't have anything to do with this."

"That's fine, I don't expect you to, all you have to do is watch. After all, that's what you like to do best, isn't it?"

He turned his back on her, and she took her phone out. She bought the camera up and set it to record on the video function, whispering into the speaker that she didn't want to be here, that she didn't want to do this, but that if she left now, Ricky would find her and hurt her. She gasped watching the first stab on her screen, Ricky kneeling between Spencer's legs and driving the blade into his back. He seemed to go into a frenzy then, the in-and-out, up-and-down motions of the knife so fast she couldn't count how many times he'd stabbed him. The torchlight bobbed erratically with each strike, and she wanted to tell him to turn it off, that it might draw attention, but if she did that, then she was aiding and abetting. She moved round to his side to get a clear shot of his face. She sobbed, the feeling of losing any control she had of this evening bringing a lump to her throat.

"Stop," she said. "Please stop. He doesn't deserve this." And it was a calculated thing to say. She'd chosen those words especially so it looked better if this should go to court. How wicked she was; how wicked Ricky had taught her to be. She'd been a willing participant once upon a time, for some bizarre reason

she now couldn't fathom. She snapped her mouth shut, thinking she may have made a mistake in talking to Ricky. He might respond and say her name. It would be recorded. As it stood, it was his word against hers that she'd even been here.

Then she remembered the staff toilets. "Oh God, I'm going to be sick."

She wouldn't if she could help it. She'd only said it to let Ricky know where she was going. Hopefully he'd realise she'd be back. All she could do now was damage limitation, and that was to wipe over the sink tap—that was the only thing she'd touched in this place without gloves on. She raced out of the room, switching the video off, legging it upstairs to the toilets. She did what she had to do and then returned to the downstairs room.

Ricky stood by Spencer's foot, the torch beam aimed at the kid's back. So much blood had seeped through his slashed-up puffa jacket, some of it in his hair, where Ricky must have sliced at his scalp when she hadn't been in the room. The amount of red took her breath away. It had seeped out of the body and onto the floor, staining it, spreading in two gloopy rivers. It had splashed behind Spencer and onto the wall beside the door, the droplets probably coming off the knife every time Ricky had raised it.

"We should go," she said.

"You're going to need an alibi." He put his balaclava back on.

"I don't need one. My dad thinks I was with you, remember? I had to come and tell you we couldn't see each other anymore." Her earlier lie had now got her in the shit. She did need an alibi. But then...why would the police even need to speak to her if she had a balaclava on and no one knew she'd been here?

"You do need one. We might have been seen together by people in town before we put the balaclavas on. We're going to have to say we were at my house at the time the party started," Ricky said.

"But what about your parents? You must be covered in blood, there's no way you didn't get any on you. They're not going to keep this quiet if they ask where the blood's come from and you tell them."

"I should have listened to you. You said there'd be too much blood with a knife."

She backed out into the corridor. "We have to go. Come on!"

She didn't wait for him. She ran out of the building, wrenching the gate open and turning left so she didn't go down the alley towards the graveyard. The sound of the gate snicking shut and then footsteps thudding behind her let her know that either Ricky followed or she was fucked because the homeless people had come after her. She reminded herself again that she had a balaclava on and gloves, although one was wet where she'd washed the tap. She kept going until she recognised the footsteps as Ricky's, then she paused in a gateway, waiting for him to catch up. She couldn't see any blood on him because his clothes were black, but she knew damn well it was there.

He took his balaclava off. "We'll go to my house. You can tell your dad you went there to tell me it was over."

"You make it sound like we were boyfriend and girlfriend." She took her own balaclava off.

"I thought we were going to be, but never mind. I'll wait for you until we're eighteen and then your dad can't tell you jack shit. He can't stop us from seeing each other then."

Bloody hell, he really thought she'd want to wait for him now he'd killed Spencer. What a deluded dickhead. She was going to have to rebuff him somehow. Let him down in a different way. But not tonight. Tonight was ensuring they had an alibi. The pair of them wandering around the streets wasn't a good enough one, even though a lot of teenagers did just that.

He turned and led the way, and once again she followed.

But this was the last time.

Chapter Twenty-Nine

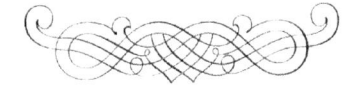

Emma hated admitting she was a liar, let alone that she was an accessory to murder. Amanda's strange acceptance of it was a far cry from the twins' reaction. It was so obvious George was trying to hold his temper at bay, and Greg observed him as though he'd have to dive in at any minute if his brother decided to unleash any anger on Emma. She didn't blame them for being arsey, but she had to make them understand *why* she'd kept her mouth shut until now.

"On the outside he looks like he wouldn't give you too much hassle. Underneath, at least when we were teenagers, he was awful. I was just as awful to be honest, like I needed some kind of outlet for my angry emotions that had sprouted up from nowhere, and it was as if I couldn't tolerate anybody at all apart from him. All I wanted to do was be with him and talk to him and hang around with him."

"Thanks a lot," Amanda muttered. "You really did hide your real feelings from me."

George sighed and gave Amanda one of his glares. "This isn't about you this time, though, is it. You've had your turn with the troubles, and we helped you, and now it's Emma's turn, so regardless of your hurt feelings, keep them to yourself until all this is over. You've clearly never had to hide what you were really feeling as a kid, otherwise you'd understand what Emma's on about."

So he wasn't angry enough with Emma not to have empathy for her. She took it that he'd maybe struggled with being a teenager, or maybe he even struggled now, as an adult, to present one side to the world when inside it was the complete opposite.

Emma continued. "And he made me laugh. Everything bad went away when I was with him, which is weird, because we did bad things, and thought bad things, and talked about bad things."

"You were each other's outlet," George said.

"I think so. He was having a hard time at home because his dad wasn't exactly earning any medals with how he treated Ricky's mum, and Gordon was the golden boy. Ricky didn't seem to fit in anywhere unless he was with me. Or so he said anyway."

"And what about you?" George asked. "What was your reason for wanting to only spend time with him? Or was it just the hormone thing?"

"I was under a lot of pressure to pass my exams. I'd always got on at school and enjoyed it, but then all of a sudden I didn't. There were too many rules, and I detested being there, but I still went because that meant I got to see Ricky every day. I love my mum and dad, don't get me wrong, but bloody hell, they had high expectations and still do. Very much keeping up with the Joneses and worrying what people think of them. They wanted me to be more like Amanda, the princess who dressed up all pretty instead of the one who preferred jeans, a T-shirt, and a hoodie."

"So you acted out." George nodded. "I get that. Why couldn't you tell someone about the murder at the time?"

"He told me what he was going to do. I said we shouldn't go that far, that talking about it was as much as I was prepared to do, but he'd already bought the knife with him. I went along with him, thinking he'd just have a go at Spencer, punch him in the face or something, not actually kill him." She shook her head. "God, the things you tell yourself because you don't want to face up to the truth."

"What happened after you followed Spencer down the alley?"

Emma told the rest of the story.

George pinched the bridge of his nose. "Look, I'm not going to pretend that you haven't naffed me off by outright lying when I asked you whether you had any secrets, but I do understand why you kept it to yourself. Good thinking on your part to record the murder, because I think that Ricky and his father knowing you had footage kept you alive."

She shuddered at the thought of them coming after her, stabbing her like Ricky had stabbed Spencer. It didn't bear thinking about, but she'd done that so many times over the years. "It's all going to come out if Clare convinces the police he was involved, and God knows what it says in the diary. My first name's been mentioned on her posts because of the McIntyres at least giving me an alibi, it's on the police file I was supposedly at their house that evening."

"The homeless bloke who got the blame. What did he say he was doing?"

"He said he'd gone past the building we were in with Spencer to meet his friend who'd been to the homeless shelter and picked up some beanie hats and gloves for them. They talked and smoked rollies for a bit, then he went back down the alley, and that was when the witness in the graveyard had seen him and assumed that all the time he'd been with his mate, he'd really been killing Spencer."

"Who was the witness?"

"Some bloke with his girlfriend."

"Didn't the police get hold of the homeless man's friend?"

"No one in the homeless community was talking to reveal who that was, but the people at the shelter said a man had come in and taken two sets of hats and gloves, but then so had several others, so effectively, it could have been any one of them. The homeless man accused of the murder only knew of him by a nickname."

"What was it?"

"Coogie or something like that. Anyway, this Coogie said he was moving on from London and making his way to Manchester."

"You'd think the police would maybe wonder if the accused was telling the truth because his alibi had conveniently fucked off and couldn't vouch for him—if he was covering up for a murder, then he'd have given himself a different alibi surely. So the bloke was convicted and put in prison?"

"Yes, but he killed himself six months into the sentence." Emma closed her eyes, hot tears burning. "So in my opinion, that's another person Ricky killed."

George nodded. "It's a right fucking mess, isn't it. So the long and short of it is you were too afraid to come forward."

"Yeah. Mr McIntyre made it quite clear what would happen to me if I ever opened my mouth."

"He was protecting his son, so you can probably understand his point of view, but if he were still alive today, then we'd be bringing him in an' all. As it is, we're going to have to speak to Mrs McIntyre and Gordon—but not tonight. There'll be enough eyes on that family once it's obvious Ricky's gone missing."

Relief pushed Emma's shoulders down. "So you're going to get rid of him, then?"

"Yeah, I don't think we've got any other choice if we want to keep you out of the nick, or worse, stop you from being the next one on his list. For now, we'll go and pick Ricky up."

"I'm sorry," Emma said.

"Let's move on, shall we?" George stood and smiled. "I'm going to have fun asking him what he's been up to."

Chapter Thirty

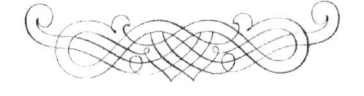

Mrs Zameen Abbasi was all for having sympathy for a grieving person, but this loud music business was too much. She was in mourning herself, her dear husband died and departed these past six months, and she imagined, like Clare, she would still grieve over a decade later, but there were ways of doing it, weren't there. Zameen understood the music, she honestly did. Clare had explained why it was turned up high, so she could properly scream-cry to get all of the emotions out of her, but even Zameen had her limits, and eleven o'clock at night was far too late to be listening to heavy rock.

She was going to have to go round there.

Far be it for her to be 'one of those neighbours', but she had no choice.

Putting on her dressing gown and doing the belt up securely, she popped her feet in her slippers and put on a woolly hat and gloves. She collected Clare's spare key from the little box on the wall by the front door, put her own in her pocket, and went out into the biting cold. Down her garden path and up Clare's, she debated whether she should go home — if the music was still on after so long, Clare must be in a very bad way tonight.

But what if she needs someone to talk to?

Zameen slid the key in the lock, wincing at how the music was even loud out here. She was surprised none of the other neighbours had phoned the police regarding the racket, but then wouldn't they be fobbed off, told to keep a noise diary and send it to the Environmental Health department at the council?

Zameen pushed the door open, preparing herself to go up to Spencer's room and switch the music off, then guide Clare into her bedroom and encourage her to go to sleep. Except Clare lay at the bottom of the stairs, her chin tucked to her chest, an arm trapped beneath her, the other sticking out in front. That wrist looked unnaturally bent, as did one of the fingers. Zameen gasped and rushed towards her neighbour, lowering to her knees so she could check for a pulse.

There wasn't one.

This brought back terrible memories of when her beloved Irfan had passed away. He'd tripped over in the living room and on his way down clipped his temple on the sharp corner of the mantelpiece shelf. It had dug in quite far and cut his skin and vein and…

She couldn't think about that now. She shuffled backwards, away from Clare, then got to her feet. Much as she didn't want to leave the poor dead woman alone—she'd much prefer to sit with her so her spirit had company—she was going to have to switch that music off before she could phone an ambulance. But should she touch anything in the house? What if this wasn't an accident? Clare had come round for a cup of tea earlier and mentioned that Ricky boy. What if…?

Zameen left the house and returned to her own so she could dial nine-nine-nine. With the shock of the discovery zooming through her body, she composed herself enough so she could talk without crying.

Chapter Thirty-One

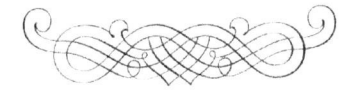

Ricky woke with the sense that someone stood beside his bed. He wasn't startled, just resigned to the fact that he was going to have to guide Gordon back to his own room. His brother had sleepwalked ever since Ricky could remember, usually during times of stress, so it was understandable that he stood in the darkness now. Except his breathing wasn't the steady in and out that Gordon usually displayed. It sounded quieter, so maybe his brother had come in, like he had when they were kids, because he'd had a nightmare and he needed someone to talk to.

Weird how, even though they were men, the old habits from their little boy lives still remained. Ricky supposed he should cut him some slack. Gordon had lost his dad, someone he'd looked up to and loved, whereas Ricky hadn't lost anything but gained some peace of mind, as had their mother.

Eyes still closed, Ricky asked, "What's the matter, Gordon?"

"It's not Gordon, it's George."

Ricky's eyes snapped open, and he went to shoot up to a sitting position, but a hand planted itself on his face and kept him down. He smelled the leather of the glove, the coldness of it against his skin sending a shiver down his spine. Or maybe that was because he had a twin in his bedroom.

"We need to have a word with you," George said. "I'm going to turn the light on so you can see to find your clothes, and I can see to find your phone. I'm going to switch it off so the last recorded location is here, but I'll take it with us because someone's going to switch it on in another location so it looks like you've left London. A train to Edinburgh sounds about right."

Ricky had heard about people getting banished by the leaders—he couldn't remember when he'd learned about it, probably when he'd been younger, but at least banishment meant he was still alive. They'd probably come to collect him to tell him off about what he'd said to Clare on that bloody Facebook group. Or had they learned somehow that he'd engineered it so his father had fallen off the railing?

Fucking hell, had Gordon got hold of them?

"What have I supposedly done?" he asked.

He blinked as the harsh light snapped on and The Brothers loomed over him, presenting as silhouettes until he'd cleared his vision enough, then he got a proper look. They had bushy beards and longish hair, both of them with baseball caps on, and gloves, and black tracksuits.

"Ah, are you going down the route of innocent until proven guilty?" George asked. "What you've *supposedly* done is killed Spencer Donaldson."

It took a moment for Ricky to process what he'd said and to ask himself whether Clare had got hold of them. Or was it Emma? If it was Clare then it had to be before he'd pushed her down the stairs, obviously, and if it was Emma… What was she playing at? Had they just taken her word for it, or had she kept a copy of the footage after all? That was something he'd planned to find out when he'd got closer to her and gained her trust, but now he might not have the chance.

But Edinburgh didn't sound so bad, and banishment meant he couldn't have done something *too* bad in the twins' eyes, because surely they'd kill him if they knew he'd committed murder.

"His mother contacted you, did she?" Ricky asked.

"Less talk and more getting dressed. And keep your voice down, you don't want your mother or brother walking in on us, do you, because that would mean they'd have to come with us, and while there's enough space in the back of the van, we could really do without having to tie them up and put cloths in their mouths to keep them quiet while we have a chat with you. And then that complicates things if they're witnesses. We'd have to threaten them to keep their gobs shut about this, maybe rough them up a bit…"

"I'll be quiet. I'll come with you."

George's teeth flashed bright amongst the hairs of the beard, and his eyes widened. He looked demonic, fucking mental, and Ricky didn't fancy being on the other end of his fists, so he'd do as he was told, make them see he was innocent—unless they'd seen the footage.

He sighed. He'd deal with that as and when.

One thing at a time.

Trembling but hoping they didn't notice, he stood and collected clean clothes from the wardrobe and drawers, and the unwanted thought popped in his head as to whether there was any point in selecting nice things.

"Do I need to pack a bag?" he asked.

George frowned. "What for?"

"You said about Edinburgh…"

"Oh, yeah. Pick enough stuff that'll fill that rucksack." George pointed to it on the floor. "And take your passport."

Ricky assumed that was because he might need it in the future if he ever wanted to go abroad—meaning, George was making it abundantly clear that he was not welcome in London again.

It was weird getting dressed in front of two big men, in such a small bedroom, too, their close proximity unnerving, as was their breathing and clenched fists which Ricky took to mean he was taking too long and testing their tempers. Dressed apart from socks, he pulled those on, slid his feet into his trainers, then folded some clothes and popped them in his rucksack. He found his passport in his bedside drawer along with his wallet and phone, which he switched off in front of George who took everything off him bar the bag, nodded, and jerked his head at the door.

Greg walked out first, and George gestured for Ricky to follow. He sensed George right at his back as the bedroom light went off. Ricky had the urge to shout out that he was being kidnapped, but despite being an arsehole in many areas of his life, he couldn't put his mother through any more trauma, so he followed Greg down the stairs, George's hand on his shoulder.

At the bottom he was allowed to put on a coat, and when they left the house and he walked down the front garden path, it felt like that coat had been stitched with thread made from the ghosts of his past—and it was heavy, dragging him down. Was that what regret felt like? He wouldn't know because he'd never felt it with regards to Spencer's murder, so maybe this regret was finally being caught.

With the unspoken threat that if he didn't do as he was told his mother and brother would suffer the consequences, Ricky glanced at the house for the last time, and then got into the back of the van. George got in there with him. Ricky placed the rucksack on the floor and sat on it, turning to look past the front seats and out of the windscreen at the houses of the street where he'd had never quite felt at home on an Estate that hadn't welcomed him like they were long-lost friends.

We should never have come back.

Chapter Thirty-Two

Mrs Mcintyre stared at Ricky and Emma who'd just this second come in through her back door and stood in her kitchen. "Oh, you've bought a girl home. And you're all flushed, look. You don't need to be embarrassed, son." She smiled at Emma. "Can I get you a drink, love?"

"No, thank you."

Ricky darted his gaze to the kitchen door. A hallway lay beyond it and another door on the right, which must be the living room. Sounds of a television drifted out, and Emma wished she'd stayed at home tonight and watched it.

"Where's Dad?" Ricky whispered.

Mrs McIntyre's shoulders slumped. "Don't be telling me you've been up to no good. Oh God, have you got her pregnant?"

"What?" Emma blurted. "No! We haven't even kissed."

"Bloody hell, Mum!"

Mrs McIntyre smiled. "Sorry, I jumped the gun a bit there. So what's the matter if you're asking where your father is?"

"Can you say me and Emma have been here all night?"

"What have you gone and done?"

"I can't tell you."

Mrs McIntyre looked him up and down, and then her eyes widened. "Is that blood dripping off your coat onto my nice clean floor? Have you hurt yourself? Where are you cut? Let me see."

Emma's legs didn't want to hold her up anymore. She pulled a chair out and sank onto it, resting her elbows on the table and balancing her forehead on one of her hands. Mrs McIntyre and Ricky stared at each other for the longest time, and then the woman's tears came, running down her face so quickly and stopping on her chin for a moment then dripping off onto her light-blue cardigan.

"Yes, I can say you were here all night," she said, "and I'll have to make sure Gordon keeps his mouth shut. He's in the living room." Mrs McIntyre turned to shut the kitchen door, then she spun back to face them and leaned on it. "As carefully as you can, get undressed. Everything off."

Ricky glanced at Emma.

Mrs McIntyre tutted. "I'm sure the girl will shut her eyes, but you need to take everything off, turning it inside out as you do it, then put it in the washing machine."

Emma shielded her eyes.

"That's it. Now wash your hands. Yes, I know you had gloves on, but wash them anyway, and then take yourself off into the shower room."

Water splashed, then footsteps pattered on the lino. What Emma imagined was a door opened and closed. Mrs McIntyre told her she could open her eyes.

"We're very lucky to have the shower room," she said. "I saved up to have it put in. There's a little toilet in there, too." Ricky's mum went over to the cupboard

above the under-counter fridge and took out a bottle of Saxo salt. She poured the lot in the washing machine drawer, selected a cycle, the digital dial showing it as thirty degrees. "I'll pop it on a hot wash when this cold one's finished. But it's salt and cold water for blood, in case you need to know for the future."

She took out a bottle of bleach from under the sink and got on with cleaning her washing-up bowl with it using a scourer, then she tackled the bloodstains on the floor. She went outside and scrubbed the garden path, then came back in and tipped the dirty water down the sink.

As she bleached that, she asked, "What did my boy do?"

Emma didn't want to say it out loud, so she took her phone out, removed one of her gloves so she could access the screen, and set the recording to PLAY. *She held the phone tight but showed the woman who paled and shook her head as though she couldn't believe what she was seeing. The horrible film ended, and Emma switched her phone off and popped it in her pocket.*

Mrs McIntyre staggered back to lean against the sink unit. "Oh my God. Oh my God. Who is the poor dead boy?"

Emma refused to respond.

The kitchen door flung open, and Gordon stood there, staring from his mother to Emma and back again. "What's going on?"

"Your brother's in the shower. He and this girl have been here all evening, do you understand?" Mrs McIntyre's voice trembled. She glared at Gordon. "Do. You. Understand?"

"Yes, Mum."

"Good boy. What have you been watching?"

He recited a list.

Mrs McIntyre looked to Emma. "Did you hear that? Remember it because that's what you watched, too."

Emma nodded then jumped when Ricky came out of the shower room with a towel wrapped around his middle. He saw his brother and groaned.

"It's fine," Mrs McIntyre said. "He'll be fine. We'll all be fine, so long as your father doesn't hear about this." She glared at Gordon. "I mean it. You mustn't tell him."

"I don't know what I'm supposed to tell him anyway," Gordon said.

"Hopefully you'll never have to know." Mrs McIntyre let out a long breath, her eyes closed.

The sound of a key going in a lock had them all staring towards Gordon, who turned to gawp into the hallway.

"And now we're all fucked," Mrs McIntyre whispered.

<hr>

Emma hadn't thought she'd be back in the building so soon, or ever, but here she was with the McIntyre family, standing on Ricky's square of tarpaulin so none of their shoes got blood on them. They all stared down at Spencer in the torchlight. Mr McIntyre had insisted he come and have a look at what had gone on for himself, and it seemed he now regretted it, his cheeks flushing, perhaps with anger.

"What was this all about?" The torch beam wobbled where his hand rose then fell. He glared at Emma. "Was this because of you? Did they both fancy you and things got out of hand? It's always a woman, isn't it? It's always their fault."

"It was nothing to do with me," Emma said. "I didn't do anything. It was all Ricky."

The torch went off, and she braced herself to be gripped up by her coat and slammed against the wall, but nothing happened. All of their breathing clashed, so uneven and ragged.

"There's nothing to stop me from telling the police this was you, girl," Mr McIntyre said. "This place is abandoned, and this kid won't be found for ages, but when the news leaks? If anyone comes round my house to accuse my son, I'll be dropping your name right in it. You'll be the one going down for this, not my lad."

"You can't," Mrs McIntyre whispered.

"Don't you tell me what I can and can't do," he said.

"No, I mean you literally can't. She filmed it. She has the video on her phone."

"Jesus fucking wept." Mr McIntyre exploded towards Emma. "Give me that fucking phone."

"No."

Surprisingly, he retreated. "You'd better keep your mouth shut. If I even get a sniff that you've told someone about what my son did, there'll be trouble."

"I won't be telling anyone," Emma said, her bottom lip trembling. "I just want to go home."

"I'll drop you off. It'll look like we all came out to take you home. Now get off this fucking tarpaulin and fold the bastard thing up. I'll have to burn that when we get back. Who even carries that around with them?"

If this situation wasn't so scary, Emma would have smiled at their thoughts matching. She waited in the corridor and then followed the family out of the building and through the yard, down to the left, all of them hurrying with their heads bent until they reached Mr McIntyre's car. The drive to her house was made in silence, Gordon's elbow digging into Emma's side in the back seat, Mrs McIntyre quietly crying in the front. The car came to a stop, and Emma got out, never so relieved to be away from someone. Mrs McIntyre and Gordon were all right, but Ricky and his dad were fucking nuts.

She let herself in through the side door and stood in the porch to take off her shoes and coat. She worried whether there was blood on it, even just a speck, so she crept into the kitchen and put it in the washing machine along with her clothes.

"Is that you, Em?" Mum called.

"Yeah."

"Is that the washing machine I can hear?"

"Yeah. I fell over on the way to my friend's house. I got mud all over me."

Mum appeared in the kitchen doorway, rolling her eyes at Emma standing there in her knickers and bra. "You always did have two left feet. I hope you didn't get Laura's mum's carpet dirty or anything."

"I didn't go to Laura's."

Mum frowned. "Oh. But you said…"

"I told a fib. I'm sorry."

"Why did you lie?"

Emma forced herself to blush. "I've got a boyfriend and I went round there for the first time tonight."

The mask of upset left mum's face, and she smiled so hard her cheeks must be hurting. "Oh my God, you don't have to tell fibs about that! Go and get your pyjamas on while I make you a hot chocolate and you can tell me all about him. And his mum. I assume she was there."

"Yeah, so was his dad and brother. I won't be a minute."

Emma ran upstairs, fighting back tears. She couldn't cry, not yet. Not until she'd spoken to Mum and weaved another web of bullshit. But it was the last one.

She promised.

Chapter Thirty-Three

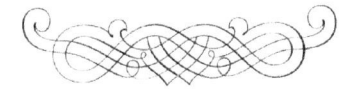

Detective Sergeant Colin Broadly stared down at the body in the hallway, and in horrifically cruel fashion, it reminded him of the day he'd stared down at his dead wife. For a few seconds, he was back in his own hallway, the shit shocked out of him, his whole world tumbling. He'd promised his boss, Nigel, that work was work and he could cope with it, but quite honestly, in this moment, he could walk out and not look back. But he wouldn't. He was going to stand here and go through the motions and tell himself that Clare Donaldson was not Libby Broadly. He was going to ask the neighbours some questions, despite the late hour. He was going to do his job. Nigel currently questioned the paramedic who'd called this scene in as suspicious, so that was one thing off Colin's to-do list.

Clare had a fresh bruise on her back that may indicate she'd been pushed.

As murders went, this one was pretty tame. No blood all over the place. Nothing broken, except maybe that wrist and finger. Mind you, inside her body might be a different matter.

So what had happened here? An argument, perhaps, that had got out of control, the other person growing angrier and angrier until they'd struck out. Or maybe it had been planned. Either way, it was a job Colin needed to get through, just like how he got through life without his wife — determined to make it to the end of the day without crying, because Libby wouldn't want him to be upset. He now lived with her in mind —

what would Libby want me to do here? What would she want me to say? How would she want me to act? That way, he could pretend she'd given him the advice for real and that she was still here somewhere, he just couldn't see, hear, or touch her.

Apparently, this was a way to navigate grief, but the twins' therapist, Vic, had advised him that while pretending Libby was still here was a good coping mechanism for now, he was only fooling himself, and at some point he'd come up against such a heavy wall of grief that it would eventually fall, brick by brick, on top of him.

But Vic didn't know how strong Colin had become. He was going to lock away all the bad things with regards to Libby and only think of the good. He was going to smile if her name came up, not cry. He was going to live the rest of his life righting the wrongs, which included finding the scumbag who'd killed this poor woman in front of him.

To give himself a head start before he spoke to the neighbours—two women who currently waited together in the house of the one who'd phoned for an ambulance—he was going to find out whether Clare Donaldson was known to the twins for any reason. Best he check from the off whether he had to steer this investigation in a direction well away from them.

He walked into the kitchen, his forensic booties shuffling on the lino, and raised his eyebrows at a SOCO who currently dusted the back door for prints. Bugger, Colin had wanted to be alone.

"I came in to see whether any prints have shown up on the door handle, in or outside," Colin lied.

"Yeah, there are partials."

"Good, good."

Colin left the room and walked past the body in the hallway, where Sheila Sutton, the crime scene manager, stood with Jim, the pathologist. He held up a finger to them to explain that he needed some air, then stepped outside, wanting to scream because Nigel stood on the path with the paramedic.

"I just need…a minute," he said to Nigel, internally cursing; now his boss was going to think he wasn't up for the job because another woman had been murdered and it reminded him too much of his wife. He scooted past the two men, cursing himself yet again because he'd forgotten to take his booties off. He'd have to put a fresh pair on when he returned inside.

Out on the pavement, which was unfortunately littered with residents in their pyjamas and a few police in uniform, Colin held in his frustration and marched up the pavement until he was finally, blessedly alone. He stood by a postbox nestled into someone's front garden wall and scanned the area for potential unwanted approaches. No one seemed to be interested in him, and despite the fact that his phone screen was going to light up when he sent a message, it was tough, he needed to get ahead of the game here. If Nigel glanced up the road and happened to question him later as to what he was doing, he could always say he was playing a game to separate his mind from the murder. The twins' former copper, Janine, had warned him he'd have to be quick on his feet when it came to thinking of excuses.

COLIN: CLARE DONALDSON. ANYONE I NEED TO BE AWARE OF?

GG: AH, HER NAME'S ALREADY COME UP FOR US TONIGHT. WHY, WHAT'S GOING ON?

COLIN: LOOKS LIKE SHE'S BEEN PUSHED DOWN THE STAIRS AT HER HOUSE.

GG: Fuck. Okay, can you take a call?

Colin: No, I'm out in her street. Can't risk being overheard.

GG: Go and sit in the car or something then. It's too much info for me to type, and we're busy.

Colin sighed and got in the passenger seat of Nigel's car, something he should have done straight off the bat as soon as he'd left the house, but his frustration levels had pushed him to walk away instead. He glanced at the garden path. Nigel and the paramedic had gone.

He selected the twins' number from his burner phone contact list and put it on speaker so he could hold the mobile out of the way on his lap.

George answered quickly.

"What can you tell me?" Colin asked.

"We've currently got a bloke with us called Ricky McIntyre who's refusing to admit to the accusation that he killed some kid years ago called Spencer Donaldson."

"Fuck. And he's related to Clare."

"She's his mother. She's got a bee in her bonnet about it being Ricky, but you'll never guess who actually brought this to our attention."

Colin didn't feel like playing games but he'd have to indulge George. "Who?"

"Emma."

"Not the one from the Suits?"

"Yep. She happened to be there when Ricky killed Spencer. She filmed it. I've seen the footage, and it isn't pretty. We've got the little cunt bang to rights, but I want him to admit it. Unfortunately, he seems to think we're shipping him off on a train to Edinburgh despite the fact I've asked him time and time again whether he killed Spencer. I'm going to let him know later that he isn't going to Edinburgh, only his phone is, if you catch my drift."

Colin nodded. "Ask him whether he pushed Clare down the stairs."

"How far into this investigation are you, because I'd have thought you'd have heard by now that she had the police round her gaff earlier; she's made allegations about Ricky online and had to give a statement."

"It's only me and Nigel here at the minute, the rest of the team haven't got to the station yet, but I'm sure that snippet will crop up within the next half an hour. What do you need me to do?"

"When it becomes obvious Ricky might be involved, steer it in the direction that he's done a runner, but keep your lot away from King's Cross until about ten in the morning so someone from our crew has got time to pop his phone on a train."

"I doubt very much we'd get that far tonight anyway, because if his phone is off until it needs to be switched back on for the train, it would be a dead end at the minute anyway. There'd be the visit to his house first, so it should all go to plan. I take it he's going to disappear in a permanent way."

"Of course he fucking is."

The line went dead, and Colin cleared the evidence of the call and the messages. He kept this phone on vibrate only and slipped it into the inside pocket of his suit jacket. It was time to go back into the house and pretend he'd got himself under control now.

He walked with purpose to the front door and stuck his head inside. Nigel stood with Jim and Sheila, and Colin cleared his throat to get their attention. They all turned his way.

"I'm probably better off going next door to speak to the neighbours," he said.

Nigel's eyes displayed sympathy over the top of his face mask, and he nodded. "Whatever you feel more comfortable with."

Colin left them to it, removed his booties to put them in a designated bag, and then nipped to the door of—he checked his notebook—a Mrs Zameen Abbasi. According to what he'd jotted down earlier on the way to the scene, the other neighbour, who'd come out to have a word with Clare about the loud music, was called Belinda Sharp. He tapped on the door, and a PC answered, letting him in and pointing to a doorway on the right. He followed Colin into a living room where the women sat nursing cups of tea on the sofa.

He held up his ID and introduced himself.

"Sit," Mrs Abbasi instructed. "Call me Zameen; we're all friends here."

"Same goes for me," Belinda said.

Zameen talked him through the discovery of the body and what she'd done and touched, but now he'd spoken to George, he was more interested in what Clare had said in the days preceding her murder—if, indeed, it *was* murder.

"Oh, she was obsessed with that man, wasn't she," Belinda said.

Zameen nodded. "Ricky McIntyre. She kept it to herself until the dad died. Verne, his name was."

"Whose dad?" Colin asked to make sure they were on the same page.

"Ricky's," Zameen said. "He was drunk and fell off a railing into the Thames. Banged his head on the way down. Ricky and his brother were there."

Colin had heard about that. His team had almost been drafted in to poke into how it might have been a murder portrayed as an accident, but witnesses at the scene, not to mention CCTV, showed the sons were too far away from their father to have pushed him and the man had sadly fallen all by himself.

"Why was Clare obsessed with Ricky?" he asked.

Belinda held her hand up as though at school. "She'd convinced herself he'd killed her son, but we all know it was that homeless man."

"Homeless man?"

Belinda explained everything, Colin jotting down notes.

"She wasn't going to go to the police until she had proper proof—she said the diary might not be enough, and the police she'd shown it to weren't interested, so she got it into her head that she was going to ask Ricky to meet up with her and she was going to record him on her phone, get him to confess."

"When did she tell you this?" Colin asked.

"After the police had been to take her statement about accusing Ricky online. She wanted to do something about it herself, quicker than the police would."

"Do you know whether she'd made contact with him and they'd arranged when to meet?"

"No, and I didn't think to ask, I just warned her that if she thought he was a killer then it might be a daft thing to meet him by herself and that it should be in a public place. I feel bad now; she obviously got him to come to her house, and now this has happened."

"I was told there was music on when you arrived, Zameen."

"Yes. She usually puts it on when she's overwhelmed and needs a good cry. She doesn't like either of us to hear her. We still get upset, though, don't we, Belinda? When the music comes on it's obvious what's happening. It had gone on for ages this time, she never usually leaves it on so late, and I'd just about had enough of it when I went round there with my spare key."

"And you found her on the floor."

"Yes. I checked for a pulse and then left the house to go home to phone the police because it was too noisy in hers."

"What time did the music start?"

"About seven," Belinda said. "So you can understand why I thought Clare was taking the piss a bit. I feel bad now, too, obviously."

"You weren't to know." Colin smiled at her. "It's human nature to blame yourself for not helping more or for not knowing what was going on, but because you knew why the music had gone on it was only natural you thought it was for a genuine reason."

"Oh God, are you saying it could've been on for another reason?"

He wasn't going to elaborate by saying a killer, possibly Ricky, had gone into the house and put the music on to drown out any arguing or screams. These two women had yet to be told that it might be murder.

"I realise you wouldn't have heard anything from seven o'clock onwards," he said, "but did you hear anything prior to that?"

"What do you mean?" Zameen asked.

"Any talking coming from next door, the doorbell going, anyone knocking to be let in…"

Belinda shook her head.

"I didn't hear a thing out of the ordinary," Zameen said. "Why do you ask?"

"If you could just bear with me for a second… Do you know of anyone who'd want to harm Clare?"

Belinda appeared startled if her raised eyebrows were any indication, then she frowned. "Unless the police spoke to Ricky and he got pissed off—sorry, annoyed—that she'd accused him of murder, then I can't think of anybody. Her daughter, that's Heidi, has distanced herself since Clare split up with her ex-husband, but she doesn't hold a grudge or anything, and she certainly wouldn't come here to hurt her mother."

"What about the ex?"

"Derek? God, no, he just got overwhelmed by Clare's preoccupation with Spencer's death—it's understandable that he needed to get away from her. Then when she found the diary, she became obsessed."

"When was this?"

"I can't remember exactly," Belinda said, "but it'll be on Spencer's Facebook page. I don't mean his personal one, I mean the one Clare created for him. It's called Justice for Spencer. She writes about things quite a lot on there."

"Thank you, that will be very helpful."

He chatted to them for a while longer, gathering information. Unfortunately, it meant he was going to have to tell Nigel about a possible suspect, Ricky, and he'd probably tell Colin to take a PC with him to Ricky McIntyre's address. But that was okay. The more time that was wasted trying to locate Ricky, the more time the twins had to dispose of his body.

Chapter Thirty-Four

Meryl didn't much like being woken up in the middle of the night to find neither of her sons had got up to answer the knock at the door. She left the bed and moved the curtain at the edge of the window to peer down. Her stomach plummeted. They were easy to see because of the nearby streetlamp, but whatever was going on that meant the police needed to be here, she didn't know, unless her suspicions had been confirmed and they'd come to ask Ricky a few questions about Verne's death.

She let the curtain fall back into place and returned to bed, getting comfortable again beneath the warmth of her thick duvet. She just had the funeral to get through and then she was out of here. No more worrying about Ricky and what he was up to. Out of sight, out of mind would be a good mantra to follow.

Another knock. She didn't want either of her boys to answer it now, and with anger burning a path through her, she got up yet again and went out onto the landing. She sat on the top step and stared down at the officers' silhouettes through the speckled glass. She'd stay here until they went away. At least then, if they kept knocking, she'd be on hand to tell Ricky and Gordon to go back to bed.

Eventually, the policeman shapes retreated, and she waited for a couple of minutes until the sound of their car disappeared. Still a bit arsey, she opened Ricky's bedroom door, determined to wake him up and ask him if he'd been up to something other than having a possible hand in Verne's death. She flipped the light on.

He wasn't in bed. It had been slept in, but he hadn't bothered making it once he'd got up. His rucksack was gone from beneath the window, and the wardrobe door and one drawer were open. She stepped in to check his bedside cabinet, incensed to find his passport had gone—incensed because he could at least have given her the heads-up that he was fucking off. But then she became more rational and really thought about it. He must have planned it this way. Had she opened the front door and the officers had come upstairs to find him, her reaction would have been genuine when they said he wasn't there. Now, she'd fucked it up by wanting answers, storming in here the way she had.

She shut the light off and closed the door, retreating to her bed. If Ricky had run then it meant this was serious and the police would be back soon. Just like she had on the days after Spencer's murder, when everyone had been speculating, she was going to have to act out another excellent performance where she appeared innocent.

She cursed her son for once again being the reason why she had to go to Wales, except this time, she looked forward to going.

Chapter Thirty-Five

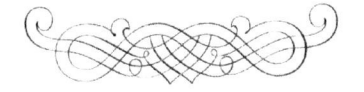

Ricky had repeated it several times: *I didn't kill Spencer*. His acting skills were pretty decent, but unfortunately for the naked man hanging from the chains in the torture room of the warehouse with a spotlight trained on him, George didn't believe him.

"We know you're lying, so you may as well just tell us the truth and be done with it." There was no way George would believe this pleb over Emma. The fear in her eyes when she'd recalled how frightened she'd been at the thought of being accused as an accessory had told him all he needed to know: she'd been brave to put on a front, she was a bloody strong person to be able to pretend like that, but inside she must have been a right old mess. He wouldn't be surprised if she was on anxiety medication.

George paced backwards and forwards in front of him. Maybe he ought to open the trapdoor to show Ricky where he was going to end up. The muffled sound of the River Thames filtered up, but when that door was open it would be so loud, especially because it tended to echo around the stone walls.

"I may as well come clean with you," George said, "to reveal a truth I've previously refused to tell you. It shows I'm willing then, doesn't it, to be open and honest. Maybe that'll give you the nudge to do the same. It wasn't Clare who told us about you, it was your old buddy, Emma."

Ricky closed his eyes for a moment and then opened them to stare at the flagstones beneath George's feet. "What did she say?"

"She didn't have to say anything, not when she had something interesting to *show* us."

"The footage."

"Aren't you a clever boy. Yeah, the footage of you killing Spencer, something you've so far professed you didn't do, but unfortunately for you, you removed your balaclava, you didn't think in your wildest dreams the girl you hung around with would video you, and you maybe didn't think that you'd look exactly the same as you did back then, just older, a little more seasoned. It's plain as day that it's you on that video. So now we've established you *did* kill Spencer, let me ask you another question. Did you kill Clare?"

The shock registered on Ricky's face before he had a chance to disguise it.

"I expect you're wondering how we know about her death. See, the thing is, we have a certain copper in our pocket, and he contacted us to ask whether Clare was known to us, then he proceeded to tell me that she was pushed down the stairs in her own home. What did you have to do it for? Was she getting too close to the truth and you panicked? We heard your father snuffed it, too. That he was drunk and fell into the river. That you and your brother were there. What did you do, convince Gordon your father needed to die? I'm speculating on that one, because according to the news articles online, neither of you were close enough to your old man to make sure he toppled, but I have a feeling you got rid of him for one reason or another."

"He hurt my mother. For years."

"Then you get a pass for bumping him off, I approve of that one. But Clare, what went on there?"

Ricky ignored him and allowed his body to go limp, closing his eyes and dropping his head down. George selected a Stanley knife from the tool table and stood in front of Ricky, staring at his thigh where the femoral artery was. This would be over so quickly if he nicked that, but despite Clare being dead, George wanted some answers as to why Spencer had been killed. He refused to believe Emma's suggestion that it had been a full stop at the end of a long line of bullying; there had to be something more. You didn't just kill some kid in your school because he got on your nerves.

"I *said*, why did you kill Clare?"

Ricky remained in place. "I needed to shut her up. She pointed the finger in my direction, so what else was I supposed to do?"

"And Spencer? Why did you off him?"

Ricky laughed and opened his eyes. "If you think you're going to get some sort of confession where I reveal how that kid made me feel, then you're wrong. You can cut me into a million pieces, you savage fucking cunt, and I'll never tell you."

"You overestimate your powers of control. There are so many ways to torture a confession out of someone—and they work in the end. Some people last days, though. I'm not on about the ones I torture. I get bored of them not giving me an explanation long before they ever want to open up to me, but think about all those people who're captured on enemy lines. Give it enough pain, they spill the beans eventually. It's okay, I've got the time and patience to play with you for a little bit longer, and if you don't tell me what I want to know, it's really not going to make a massive difference to my life. I'll forget you the second you take your last breath. You're nobody to me. But I did wonder whether you'd want me to pass on your reasons to your mother before I kill *her*."

Ricky's head shot up, his eyes flashing open to glare at George. "Don't you *dare* touch my mother."

George's laughter reverberated around the cold room. He made another mental note to buy some halogen heaters. Actually, before he forgot completely... He placed the Stanley knife on the table and brought up the Amazon app and had a nice browse, leaving Ricky to seethe and snort and heavy breathe. George pressed the ORDER NOW button, glancing over at his brother to find him sitting on one of the fold-out chairs beside the tool table, immersed in some game or other on his phone.

"That's the heaters ordered," he said.

Greg looked up and smiled. "Thank God for that, it's nippy in here." He lowered his head and continued his game.

Ricky stared from Greg to George, his frown scoring deep lines between his eyebrows. "How the fuck can you be so casual when I'm hanging here with no fucking clothes on?"

Without realising it, Ricky had given George an insight to his mental state. He didn't like having his dick and nuts exposed, most men didn't, but he actually thought he was more important and warranted more attention than George and Greg had given him.

George popped his phone away. "*You* might be the most important person in your fucked-up world, sunshine, but you're not the most important in ours. We've got things we ought to be doing outside of this little meeting here—as you've already gathered, I've just bought some heaters. I saw a few other nice things on there, like craft knives, which reminded me I'd not long been holding a Stanley knife and that I really ought to be getting on with giving you a few cuts."

He moved closer to the tool table and held up a transparent spray bottle containing clear fluid. He pulled the trigger, which sent a misty shower of liquid into the air. George sniffed the scent.

"Shit, that's made me hungry now." He smiled at Ricky. "That's okay, blood and gore don't put me off my food. We'll order something to be delivered at our place once you're in the river."

George picked up the Stanley knife in one hand and gripped Ricky's ear with the other. He pulled it out to stretch the skin between the ear and the head, then rested the blade there. Ricky was sensible and didn't dare move. Maybe he thought George was messing with him, that he wouldn't really cut his ear off, but he'd better think again.

George sliced slowly, expecting Ricky to jolt now the pain had kicked in, so he held the ear tighter. Ricky wrenched his head away which meant the ear ripped rather than sliced. George let it go, leaving it dangling from the lobe, the only remaining piece attached. He stepped back to admire the blood flow and how the ear jostled and wobbled, Ricky screaming with his eyes shut, his hands forming rhythmic starbursts then fists.

George collected the spray bottle and stood there waiting for Ricky to shut up. The bloke sobbed, snot streaming over his lips. Eventually, things got a bit quieter, and George hid the bottle behind his back. Ricky opened his eyes to blink away the tears, and he stared at George who gave him one of his best smiles as he took two steps closer.

While he maintained eye contact with their victim in an attempt to keep Ricky's focus on him, George said, "This is going to sting."

Before Ricky could turn his head to see what George was holding, George pulled the trigger of the spray bottle, sending a speckled sheet of white vinegar onto the ear wound. Ricky screamed blue murder while once again George thought about food—fish and chips. Ricky did a weird dance on the chains, throwing his head backwards and forwards, the dangling ear flapping and slapping against his neck. It was getting on George's last nerve so he ripped it off, Ricky's new scream so loud it had George gritting his teeth. Ear placed on the floor to one side of the trapdoor, George walked around to the opposite side so he could slice off the other one. He did it quickly, couldn't be arsed to draw that out, and popped it on the floor beside its twin.

Ricky choked on his own spit because he cried so much. George dipped the Stanley knife in a bucket of soapy bleach water then placed it on a folded piece of kitchen roll on the tool table. He had another quick look on Amazon, giving in and putting the craft knives in his basket, moving to the 'RELATED TO ITEMS YOU'VE VIEWED' page.

Fluffy bobbles, PVA glue, tubes of glitter, and packets of felt in different colours. He smiled at the algorithm thinking the craft knives were for something innocent, then nipped to his previous orders so he could buy some more white vinegar as he had a feeling he might use a lot of it in the future.

Stanley knife in hand again, he made slow precise cuts all over Ricky's torso, amusing himself by spraying each wound with vinegar. This time, while they were still wet, he picked up a pot of salt and sprinkled it over the cuts. He blanked out Ricky's screeching, getting annoyed because the stupid bastard wouldn't keep still. Despite knowing he couldn't get away from George and the salt, he still tried to swing around to prevent him from putting it on.

Next he sliced off Ricky's cock, just because he could, and sprayed it liberally, more than necessary, drenching the circular gash so much the liquid, pink with blood, dribbled down his inner thighs and over the cuts there. George put the Stanley knife down and filled his palm with salt, then he slapped it over the dick mess. Stanley knife in his hand again, he waited patiently for the racket to stop. He was surprised Ricky hadn't passed out yet.

Ricky continued screaming.

George had had enough. He retracted the blade then popped it on the table so he could unlock and open the trapdoor. The rush of cold air along with the pulsing noise of the river infiltrated the room, shocking Ricky out of his self-indulgent pity party. He stared down at the churning water, at the froth on the crests, and while George had his attention, he kicked the ears and cock into the depths. He grabbed the Stanley, released the blade, and swiped in the region of the femoral artery, cutting deep.

He'd hit the right spot on the first go. Ricky's horrified screech at the sight of blood pissing out of the hole prompted George to grin widely. He stepped back to watch the man bleed out and, once Ricky had gone limp, he checked the security monitor on the wall for anyone in the vicinity, then got on with chopping him up using his hedge cutter saw.

Ricky was no longer a menace or a threat.

It remained to be seen whether the same could be said for Meryl and Gordon.

Chapter Thirty-Six

She wasn't as worried about seeing Ricky again because this time was definitely the last. Everyone had been spoken to at school about Spencer, who'd been found by the owner of the building two weeks after he'd been reported missing. Ricky had asked if they could get together because he had something to tell her. She hoped he wasn't going to walk into a police station and confess.

She waited for him in the tree clearing, her phone in her hand in her pocket, the camera app open, ready to record at the push of a button. She didn't trust him not to hurt her, and if it seemed like he was going to, then she'd whip her phone out so he'd know exactly what she was doing. She stood close to the opening, so if she had to run she could.

He came jogging over the grass, a beanie hat pulled low, his hands in his pockets. He brushed past her to go and stand in the clearing, and she turned to look at him, although she worried his dad would come along any minute and do something horrible to her.

The past fortnight had been absolutely awful. She'd had a nightmare every night and had to keep it to herself otherwise Mum would ask what she was worrying about. Each day there had been no news about the body had been torture. She'd kept thinking of those flies in the building and how they'd probably laid eggs in the cuts on the back of Spencer's head. She'd imagined they'd turned into loads and loads of maggots so it looked like millions of them had hatched and were spilling out of his brain. And she thought about what he'd said: I want my mum.

Unable to stand seeing Ricky's messages popping up, she'd made out she'd lost her phone. She'd switched it off and shoved it under her bed in a box. She couldn't bear to even see it now. Mum and Dad had taken a bit out of their savings and bought her a different brand. Ricky must have realised she'd changed her number because she hadn't replied to his texts: he'd stopped her in school and let her know he'd been messaging, which was when he'd told her he had to tell her something.

"What did you need to tell me?" she asked.

"We're moving away."

"Where?"

"Funny enough, Wales."

"How come? Has your mum left your dad?"

"No, he's coming with us. He reckons it's best we get out of London because of what happened."

"So I'm the only one left to take the blame, you mean?" She panicked, her heartbeat fluttering. "What's he going to do, wait until you've got settled and then do an anonymous phone call, giving the police my name?"

"You're not thinking straight. Why would he do that when you've got the video?"

She took a deep breath to steady her nerves. "You should never have done it. I told you not to, didn't I?"

"I couldn't help it. It was like this compulsion."

"What happens when you get another 'compulsion'? Who will it be next? Your dad? Me?"

"I'd be pretty stupid to come back here from Wales to murder you. It'd leave more of a trail."

"You could do it now and no one would know. You could leave me by the trees. I might not be found until tomorrow. Likely by a dog."

"I don't want to kill you."

"You're lying. You're probably going to come out with some bollocks about killing me if I ever tell anyone about the video."

"Think what you like."

"Oh, I will."

She walked out of the clearing, shitting herself, waiting for him to jump on her back like he had with Spencer. It would be so easy for him to march her back into the clearing and stab her to death. Maybe that's what she deserved. She'd been with him when he'd robbed shops and lock-ups. She'd stood by and done nothing during the times she'd been with him when he'd bullied Spencer. She'd jumped over walls when they'd almost got caught for this and that. All because…what? She couldn't even say it was so she belonged or she felt wanted, because she'd had all of that from her family. Still did and always would.

She didn't understand who she'd become when she'd hung around with Ricky, but thank God she'd retained some semblance of right and wrong. If she hadn't, and she'd been completely mesmerised by him, God knows what she would have done. That night he'd killed Spencer, would she have joined in if he'd brainwashed her to? She'd like to say not, but she really didn't know the answer to that.

Chapter Thirty-Seven

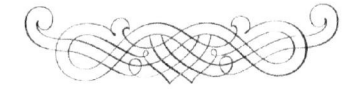

Meryl had expected to be woken up yet again by the police, but she *hadn't* expected to open her eyes to George standing over her, tapping a rhythm with his finger on her shoulder, in her *bedroom*, no less.

"Wakey-wakey," he said. "I know it's early, but we really need to have a little chat. You might already be aware that Ricky's gone missing, and that's because he killed Clare Donaldson and her son, Spencer. No, no, there's no need to protest his innocence because he's already confessed. What's left to determine now is whether you and your other son can be trusted to remain free. I hear you were at least sympathetic towards Emma when you lot inspected Spencer's body or whatever the fuck you were doing that night — maybe you didn't believe Ricky when he told you what he'd done so you had to go there to make sure for yourself. Whatever, it doesn't much matter now, does it."

"Ricky's a law unto himself," she whispered. "He was never like Gordon who did as he was told. Ricky always went his own way, like his dad, but there's one thing I can say about him is that he loved me. That's why he killed his dad, did you know that? He didn't say it to me outright, but I know it was him."

Her heart rate had increased so much, flutters flickered in her chest, and she worried she might not be able to breathe if he kept staring at her like that for much longer. He was scary, this mountain of a man, but she knew the rules about leaders, and if she wanted any chance of going back to Wales and Damien, she was going to have to throw her son to the wolves. There was no saving Ricky anyway, she didn't think, so she may as well have a good go at saving the other.

And herself.

"I'm not going to beg you to let me be free." She sat up and pushed the covers off, standing and going to her wardrobe as though George didn't frighten her at all. If she'd learned anything from living with Verne it was to not show fear. It only fuelled these types, gave them some sort of warped satisfaction. "You've probably already made up your mind what's going to happen to me, and I'm buggered if I'm going to get on my knees with my hands pressed together for anyone, not again. I suppose Greg's with Gordon."

George nodded.

"I'll ask you not to hurt him and hurt me instead, if that's where this is going. He was only twelve when the Spencer business happened, still so young—too young to have to go through what he did, to have to keep such a horrible secret because his brother couldn't keep his hands off a knife."

She sat on the bed to get dressed. Weirdly, she didn't give a flying fuck that George stood there. The days of being a prude about her modesty were long gone. She had more important things to think about now, clearly. The chickens had come home to roost, and they were noisy inside her head, flapping their wings and squawking.

To drown them out, she raised her voice. "Spencer didn't deserve what happened to him, but me and Gordon didn't deserve what Ricky had done, and we certainly didn't deserve having to live with the knowledge that he was a killer. I was prepared to go to the police, you know, for Ricky's sake, to get him put away and be given the help he needed, but Verne wouldn't let me. He drove us all down to that fucking building and made us stand in front of the body, saying we were all in it up to our armpits now, so there'd be no police."

She lifted her arms to take off her pyjama top, and George had the decency to look away. She popped a bra on and then a jumper. She removed her bottoms and switched them for knickers and jeans.

"You can turn back now." She pulled on a pair of socks. "And you don't need this confession, I can see by your face you've worked it all out already."

"Our mother would have protected us just the same way," he said. "She'd have thought about going to the police because it was the right thing to do, but like you, she would never have done it, even if there *wasn't* a man telling her she couldn't. She'd have carried the secret to her grave."

"I was going back to Wales after the funeral. I made a nice home for myself there. Met a new bloke and was seeing him on the side, and you can take that disgusted look off your face, because until you stand in my shoes, you can never understand what I went through with Verne. I don't care that you're judging me."

"I'm not, it just brought back a memory from the past, that's all."

"To do with your mother?"

He ignored her, so she put on a pair of trainers.

"If you want me to tell you that me and Gordon should be allowed to go back to Wales, then okay, I'll tell you that, but like I said, I won't beg for you to let us go. I've often imagined being caught by the police for being involved with Spencer's death, going to prison to pay for my part in hiding the truth, but never in a million years did I think it would be you who turned up."

"Why have you put trainers on?"

"Just in case you have a mind to take us out of here. I assume Gordon will be going, too. Like, it would be better that the whole family was wiped out. No more waggling tongues to worry about. You'll leave Emma alone, won't you?"

He nodded.

"Good, because that poor girl was traumatised by my son, not only by killing Spencer in front of her, but when we came back to London."

"I know."

"Get her some therapy or something. You can bet your life she needs it."

"Do you fancy making us a cuppa?"

Meryl relaxed somewhat, although this could be the cat playing with the mouse. "No, I don't as it happens, but I will."

She led the way downstairs, pleased to see Gordon unharmed sitting at the kitchen table beside Greg who looked at his brother and shook his head. Meryl had no idea what that little interaction was about and didn't give a fiddler's fuck, but she *should* care, especially if it meant Gordon got hurt, but she was so tired. Verne's death had pleased and mortified her at the same time. She mourned the lost years when she could have run away long before Spencer was killed, because she'd known back then exactly what kind of man she'd married, but she'd stayed for the children—and in the hope Verne would change back to who he'd been when they'd first got together. Except he hadn't, he'd got worse with every passing week, and she'd been stuck in a rut, and then Spencer's murder had sealed her future.

She made the tea in an eerie silence that brought on goosebumps, the hairs on the back of her neck standing up. Now she had a moment to process the fact that the twins were in her house, and putting two and two together from what George had said in her bedroom, Ricky hadn't legged it at all. She passed the cups around and then sat beside George, opposite Gordon who stared at her with guilt in his eyes—he'd thrown Ricky to the wolves, too, when talking to Greg, had he? She didn't blame him.

"So is this our last cuppa before you march us somewhere and kill us?" she asked.

Greg shook his head. "No, it's the time when my brother gets to tell you that if you open your mouth about any of this he'll likely cut your tongue out before he kills you. It's when my brother says you can go to Wales and start again, but he'll come and find you if he has to, if word gets back either of you two have been sharing little whispers. From what we've learned, you two were roped into the Spencer business, and as we know you're capable of keeping a secret, because you've done it for years already, I think we're safe enough to let you go, don't you? You fuck off after the funeral, understand?"

Meryl nodded. "I'm too exhausted to bring any more trouble to our door. I just want to live the rest of my life in peace. What do you want me to do about Ricky? Phone the police in a day or two and report him missing?"

"I suspect the police will have visited to speak with you long before that. Probably in a couple of hours, actually, when they think it's a respectable time to knock on your door."

"I'm surprised you're still here then."

"It's fine. We already know which policeman is going to come and speak to you, and he'll give us a warning that he's on his way. He came earlier with a PC, but no one answered the door."

Meryl waved off his words. "I don't want to know the ins and outs. We'll do what we've always done and maintain we don't know anything about Spencer. I expect we'll be asked about Clare, but we'll cross that bridge when we come to it. I suppose you want me to thank you for letting us go."

George stared at her. "That would be appreciated, yes."

"Then thank you."

And that was all she was going to say by way of gratitude. There was no way she'd let any man see her true emotions again, not even Damien.

Chapter Thirty-Eight

Emma had been informed about Meryl and Gordon. On one hand she was pleased they were being allowed a reprieve like she was, but on the other, she worried that at some point down the line, one of them would crack. There was nothing to say *she* wouldn't crack either, but she'd pep-talked herself that she had managed it for years so far, so she could do it for years more. The worst was already over really, the fear of being caught for Spencer's murder, but this time the police were convinced they had the right person. Ricky's name had been splashed online for the past few days, especially on the local Facebook group, and a woman called Zameen had explained on Spencer's page that she had admin privileges, therefore, she had the sad job of passing on the news that Clare had possibly been murdered by her son's killer.

Emma sat in the French Café, waiting to have a chat with someone she didn't particularly want to see, but it was a conversation that needed to be had. She caught sight of the woman walking past the window and then entering. Mrs McIntyre glanced around, and when her gaze landed on Emma, her cheeks turned a little red. Emma gestured that she'd already bought two pots of 'tea for one' which meant they'd get two cups each. She'd also bought slices of chocolate fudge cake, remembering Mrs McIntyre used to make her own version. Ricky used to sneak out of the house at night with a fat slice when they met after school and they shared it between them.

The unexpected memory stung her eyes.

Mrs McIntyre came over and sat opposite Emma. She took off her coat and draped it over the back of her chair, removing her gloves and putting them in her handbag which she placed on the floor. She stared at the tea and cake. "Well, this is all very nice, isn't it."

She sounded uncertain, and Emma felt sorry for her.

"I used to love your cake when I was a kid," she said. "Ricky brought me some."

Mrs McIntyre tutted. "Little thief. I knew it was him even though he denied it."

"He wasn't all bad, you know," Emma said.

"I know."

"And I was just as bad as him at times, even though people weren't aware of it."

"I don't want to know what you got up to with him." Mrs McIntyre poured some tea and took a sip. She continued to hold the cup while staring into the middle distance behind Emma. "It was you, wasn't it, who told the twins."

Emma nodded. "I couldn't risk Ricky not putting me in the shit. As soon as he started communicating online with Clare, I panicked. I'm not sorry I did it, but I am sorry if it hurt you."

"No, it needed to be done. Between me and you, I think he orchestrated his father's death, and he most definitely killed Clare. I shall grieve the good parts of the child and man he was, but as for the rest of him…"

"I gave him the phone I'd used to video the murder, and I said it was the only copy, but I lied. I have more."

Mrs McIntyre swivelled her eyes in Emma's direction. "If that's your way of telling me you have insurance, I don't blame you, and I'm sorry to say it's worthless where I'm concerned. It's already come out that Ricky's suspected of killing Spencer, so the proof of it on film isn't going to make much of a difference. People already believe what they want to believe. If I were you I'd get rid of it. If it ever gets in the wrong hands, it's proof you were there, your voice is on it, and I would hate for you to go down for something you'd felt forced to watch."

That was the answer Emma had wanted to hear. "I will."

They chatted for a while longer, Emma giving Mrs McIntyre a few funny stories about Ricky so she at least had something to think about fondly when it came to her son, then they parted ways,

Mrs McIntyre to prepare the last-minute bits and bobs for her husband's funeral tomorrow, Emma to go to the Suits because she had a back-to-back afternoon and evening shift.

It was good to return to normality.

Or as normal as she'd ever be anyway.

Chapter Thirty-Nine

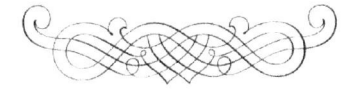

The thirty-year-old new owner of French Café, Leanora Archambeau, cleared the table the two women had just vacated. She came from Lille in France, moving here to open her business plus be with the man she'd met online, Tommy Coda. Except things hadn't turned out quite as she'd expected. In front of a monitor screen, Tommy had been charming, sweeping her off her feet, offering her a chance of security and love. She had no one left in France, hence why she'd made the decision to start again in England. He'd let her know that a café was for sale, and she'd bought it. The flat above came with it, and she hadn't rented it out when she'd moved in with Tommy, a sixth sense telling her to leave it vacant. Thank heaven she had, because he'd soon shown his true colours in the form of trying to control her.

She'd left him and contemplated going back to Lille with its beautiful architecture that lit up at night. The bars and restaurants. The Flemish stew in her favourite eatery that she'd still yet to perfect herself, oh, and the creme brûleé, the finest she'd ever eaten, and the snails. But she'd come to love the East End, this way of life, how most people were so rough and ready but friendlier than she could have imagined, so returning to a life in France wasn't on the cards when it really should be. She'd be safer there, but why should she run away when for the most part she was happy in England?

She carried the tray with the teapots, cups, and side plates on it to her little kitchen out the back. She made all the cakes herself, but a young lad came in to fill the baguettes each morning and make the sandwiches. She left the tray on the side for the young girl, Sally, to deal with when she came back from collecting her wages in the office. Leanora didn't like leaving the café unattended for long, so she went back out there.

How odd. All the customers had gone, the place completely empty apart from a man in a balaclava who stood on the other side of the counter with a shotgun pointed in her direction. He must have ushered everyone out silently, and quickly, because she'd only been in the kitchen for a matter of seconds.

She dared to look away from him, outside, to where one of her customers must have fallen over in her haste to get out. She sat on the pavement, her skirt having ridden up past her knees to reveal scrapes on them.

"Close the blinds, there's a good girl," the man said. "I've already locked up, and if you were thinking of making a run for it out the back, I wouldn't bother because someone's out there with your little washing-up girl. Cute thing, isn't she."

Leanora's stomach flipped, and she inhaled a deep breath, doing as she'd been told, her last sight of outside a dribble of blood as it meandered down the woman's shin. Would there be more blood spattered in her beautiful café in a minute? Would the man use his shotgun?

"I expect you want to know what I want," he said, "and it likely isn't what you think. Come and sit down with me and I'll explain."

She eyed him warily as she sat opposite him at the nearest table. What he said stunned and frightened her, but considering he had a weapon and he sounded sincere when he said he'd kill her if she didn't obey him, she didn't have much choice.

"You're not going to be a snitch and tell the twins," he informed her. "In exchange for your cooperation, I won't kill you." He smiled. "I can't say fairer than that, can I?"

To be continued in *Raton*,
The Cardigan Estate 38

Printed in Great Britain
by Amazon